THE HIDDEN

SHADOWED WINGS BOOK 1

IVY ASHER

Edited by Polished Perfection

Cover Design by Rainy Day Artwork

For the incredible readers who give new authors, and their books, a chance. Thank you for being dream-makers.

1

I'm shoved against a wall as soon as I clear the doorway, and lips seal to mine. The kiss is hurried, a little messy, but I can work with that. I grind my hips forward, and the hard bulge in his pants protrudes against my lower stomach. I reach down and start to undo the button on his jeans. I moan as Trevor—shit, I think that's his name, or was it Turner?—runs his hand under my shirt and cups my breast with a firm squeeze. His tongue swirls with mine as I try to recall what he said his name was when he approached me at the bar. All I can really remember was the brown scruff dusting his jaw, muscles, and the hint of his farmer's tan peeking out from the sleeve of his t-shirt.

I take over the kiss, modeling for him exactly what I like. I dive into the memory of when he came to talk to me, and dig through it for his name.

"Your boyfriend's been in the bathroom a long time," a tan, brown-eyed, brown-haired man tells me, pointing to the helmet sitting in the seat next to me.

I finish the bite of food in my mouth and then run my gaze up the stranger's lean but nicely muscled body. I take a discreet inhale of the air around me and pick up a distinct pine and soil scent. He's a wolf shifter. He gives me a knowing smile, and it's clear he's already picked up the same olfactory hints from me. I reach out and lift my helmet off the seat and place it on the polished wood of the bar I'm sitting at. I don't bother correcting the boyfriend comment. I'm decked out from head to toe in riding armor, and the helmet's obviously mine. He's either stupid or shit at opening lines; either way, he's pretty to look at and currently exactly what I'm looking for.

I take another bite of my burger as Tan and Pretty *sits down next to me. I unzip my jacket and shrug it off, exposing the gray ribbed tank top I'm wearing underneath and a lot more skin. He takes another deep inhale, and his arm brushes against mine. I'm just a shade lighter than him, but I have my father to thank for the extra dose of melanin and not the sun. My grandmother said he was from some island somewhere, although it was easier to sit through a bikini wax than to get her to be more specific than that. She never liked talking about him much.*

Travis, or whatever the fuck his name is, tries to take control and bites at my bottom lip a little too hard. It yanks me from my wandering thoughts. I growl at him and then return the favor, and he hisses at me. I'm tired of this freshman make out session that's going on. I want to fuck, shower, and get a little sleep before I need to get back on the road, and Tyler is not being nearly as aggressive as he was at the bar. I want a hot hook up, not a slow and sensual lesson in the merits of the karma sutra.

I suck on his tongue and muscle myself away from the wall I'm pressed against. I flip our positions and slam him back. The yellowing plaster of the wall cracks a little, but I doubt the manager will notice; this motel room isn't exactly a five star establishment. I grab Tate's hands and direct them to my ass, and then I reach down and rub at his hard length which is, annoyingly, still in his pants. I kiss him harder, but

2

instead of the growl and aggressive response that I'm hoping for, Tristan stiffens.

I pull back to look at him, and irritation flashes through me when his eyes aren't filled with heat like they were at the bar or when he was just feeling me up.

"I don't like dominant play," he informs me.

I stare at him dumbfounded for a couple of seconds. "Then you shouldn't pick up chicks more dominant than you," I challenge.

"I didn't think you were. You were pretty quiet and went along with my lead back at the bar," he counters.

"Yeah, because I was eating and didn't give a shit about whatever the fuck you were talking about." I separate from him and shake my head as I walk over to the door and open it.

"Are you kicking me out?" he asks, shocked.

"I wanted a good fuck, but at this point, my hand is more likely to give me that than you are," I answer simply and motion out the open doorway.

He stares at me openmouthed for a few beats as his eyes grow more and more incredulous. "I should have fucking known you'd be some alpha bitch when you got on that butch-ass motorcycle and brought me here," he accuses, grabbing his shirt from the floor and pulling it on.

My eyes narrow with anger. "That butch-ass bike is a Ducati XDiavel S, and she feels better between my thighs than I'm sure you ever would have. Bye, Troy, wish I could say it was nice to meet you."

"My name is James," he barks at me and then stomps out the door, mumbling something about how I probably don't even like men. He makes a beeline for his shitty truck, and I slam the door, leaning back against it with a huff. *James? I could have sworn it started with a T.*

I shrug it off as irritation and anger pump through me. I

can feel my wolf wanting to respond, and I take a couple of deep breaths to try to calm the both of us down. As much as she wants to rip out of me like the big bad alpha bitch that she is, I'm a fucking latent. No matter how much I try to shift, it just doesn't happen. The failure to do what should come naturally to me as a shifter hurts me and the animal that prowls underneath my skin, but I've learned to accept that it is what it is and there isn't shit I can do about any of it.

I thumb the large moonstone ring that I wear on my middle finger. It was my mother's, and I always feel close to her as I rub the same metal wrapped around my finger that was once wrapped around hers. I haven't taken it off since my grandmother gave it to me at fifteen, and playing with it or touching it in some way has become like a soothing tic. A truck engine roars to life, and the sound of tires kicking up gravel resonates just on the other side of the door.

The peeling wallpaper and obnoxious floral bedspread of the motel room are suddenly all I can see, and I try not to cringe. I was fine to get my orgasm on in here, but now the thought of staying in this place for the night makes my skin crawl. I grab my jacket off the back of the chair that's tucked into a small desk with a cracked top. The leather and the quilt stitching of my jacket hug me tightly, like the old friends they are, as I shove one arm into a sleeve, then the other, and zip it up. I grab my pack and helmet and head out.

"Well, Gran, it looks like it's just me and you again," I announce, as I strap my helmet on and make my way back to my bike. I power up my GPS as I straddle my motorcycle, and my thighs and lower back give a twinge of protest. Gran, of course, doesn't answer since she's in an urn in my backpack, but just like touching my mother's ring soothes me, talking to Gran while I take this trip helps me feel a hell of a lot better about it. The engine of my bike roars to life under me, and I pat the pack on my back reassuringly.

Gran always hated that I loved vehicles of the two-wheeled variety as opposed to the four-wheeled options, but something about the wind as it rushes past me sends my soul flying. I've been hooked on bikes since shop class when we were tasked with building one my sophomore year of high school. Even though Gran put up a fuss about it, I could always see a gleam of longing in her eyes when I talked about my love of speed and what it felt like to cut through the wind on one. She grumbled, but she never did stop me from saving up my money and buying my first bike.

I take off out of the parking lot, careful not to eat it on the gravel, and head back out toward the highway. I have about four hours of easy road ahead of me before I reach the final destination of this four-day road trip. I was hoping for a solid distraction so I could put things off a little longer, but the hard cock between my thighs I was hoping for clearly didn't work out. I merge on the highway and pick up speed as I get lost in my thoughts.

"Miss Umbra—"

"Falon, just call me Falon," I correct as I stare absently at the large cherrywood table I'm sitting at.

"Falon, did your grandmother ever discuss with you her preferences when it came to her remains?" the suited and booted lawyer asks me, his voice soft and bleeding sympathy.

"No," I answer hollowly and try to fight the melancholy sitting on my chest like a rock. I can't believe she's gone. I mean Gran was old. She had a full and, as far as I can tell, relatively happy life, but I just never really pictured myself without her. Without a tether.

"Your grandmother asked that her ashes be spread in Pinion, Alberta. It's a small town just over the Canadian–United States

border. She has an address listed here," he tells me and slides a piece of paper across the table.

He starts talking about my gran's house and her assets, but I tune him out to stare at the stark white paper with the black typed address. I've never heard of Pinion, Alberta, let alone heard Gran ever talk about it or whatever exists at the numbers sitting on the paper in front of me. I didn't think she was from a place like the small mountain town in Colorado where I grew up; I always got the impression Gran was city forged. My parents died when I was five, and ever since then, it's been Gran and me against the world. Now it's just me.

I shake away the sad memories and focus on the road in front of me. Miles blur by, and the next thing I know, the smooth female voice of my GPS tells me I'm only twenty miles away from my destination. I'm on a winding mountain road that seems to be nothing but switchbacks, and I'm having fun leaning into each turn and pushing my bike and myself to see just how much speed we can take. But with each mile I fly through, the more it feels like a boulder is resting on my sternum. Trees flash past me, and I can't help but dip back into all the curiosity I have about this place.

Gran didn't like talking about where she came from. That subject, and my dad, were pretty off limits, but the closer I get to the address that Gran left, the more I wonder if this is where her home pack lived. Gran wasn't latent like I am. She'd talk about shifting with longing and fondness, but whenever I'd ask her to shift, she'd become morose; she'd wave it away and say those days were behind her. She seemed almost relieved when my wolf couldn't complete the transformation.

I sniff at the air as much as I can with my helmet on, but I don't smell wolves or any other shifters for that matter. The crisp mountain air is cool and laced with moisture. I can smell snow on the breeze, and I really hope wherever I'm going has a place to crash for the night, or it could be a cold drive back to the last town I passed. I turn down a small road I would have never noticed on my own; thank fuck for Google Maps. I drive slowly and cautiously down the hard packed dirt path until the posh feminine voice announces, "You have arrived."

I pull into a clearing that has a small stone cabin sitting in the center. The road I'm on ends abruptly, and I stop and step off my bike. I stretch my back and legs out and wait to see if anyone is going to come out and greet me from the small little house. No one does, and after staring at the house and surrounding unkempt grass for a couple minutes, I conclude that it's empty. My gaze travels around, taking in the trees and the patches of tall grass and weeds. I'm not sure what to think about this place, but it's clearly not home to Gran's pack—or anything else, it seems.

I pull my backpack off, and my heart drops as I unzip it and pull out the urn holding Gran's ashes.

"Well, Gran, we're here," I announce as I unwrap the plastic protecting her in my bag. "I'm not sure why this place was where you wanted to be, but I guess it's only right that you kept those answers to yourself; fuck knows you did enough of that when you were alive, too."

I can practically hear her telling me to *watch my language*, and I give the urn in my hands a sad smile.

"Love you, Gran," I tell her as I walk away from the road and out into the clearing.

I look for a good spot for her and start to move toward a patch of dandelions that are in the wispy, make-a-wish stage of their lives. Out of nowhere, a white light flashes all around me, and I'm suddenly airborne, being thrown back with g-force like speed. Pain sizzles through my body, and I'm pretty sure I was just electrocuted by some invisible fucking force field. I slam into a tree behind me, and I can feel my bones breaking upon contact. I crumble to the ground, the smell of burnt skin and hair filling my nose. A whimper escapes me, but I'm broken and unable to make more sound than that.

My vision blurs and then comes into focus. Blades of grass solidify in my view, but beyond that, I can just make out my smoking hand. My mother's ring is black, and there's a brutal crack down the center of the stone. Anguish bleeds into me and ripples through the pain flooding my system. The last thing I see is the ring breaking apart and crumbling into nothing on my finger before everything goes black.

2
_____

Fresh air clears my senses as I come to. I feel groggy and surprisingly pain free. Wind whips past my face, and I revel in the feel of it. I shake away the disconnected feeling I'm currently experiencing and look around to find I'm surrounded by blue sky and wispy clouds.

What the hell? Did I die?

I flash through the sky and pull my wings closer to my body so I can fall into a fast dive.

Wings?

Confused panic crashes into me, and I come all the way to my senses. *What the fuck is going on?* I'm in the sky, the motherfucking sky, and I have wings. *Wings!* My strong black wings flare out, and I go from a dive into a soar. I scream internally, and a terrifying screech comes out of me at the same time.

Holy shit, I'm a dragon! How the fuck am I a dragon?

I look around, and shock filters through my excitement and disorientation. I'm soaring over cliffs that are a reddish-purple, and not because the setting sun turned them that color, they just happen to be reddish-purple mountains. There are patches of trees and other greenery speckled about, and I know right away that I am not surrounded by the Rocky Mountains anymore. I'm a fucking dragon, somehow flying through the sky, in a place I've never seen before, and I have no idea how any of it is happening.

A glittering light catches my eye, and I realize it's a lake of some sort. I have the sudden drive to see if I can catch what I look like in the reflection of the water. Just as that thought flashes through my mind, I feel myself lean in that direction and give a couple powerful flaps of my massive wings to propel me exactly where I want to go. *It seems I'm a narcissistic dragon.* I ride the wind toward the sparkling lake and try to figure out how my dragon body just seems to know how to do this.

I'm so overwhelmed by colors and smells and the feel of my new form that I can't seem to process anything. All I can think of is the sight of my mother's ring disintegrating on my hand, and I just know instinctively that somehow this is all connected. When my wolf—dragon, I correct myself, because it's clear now that I am most definitely *not* a fucking wolf shifter— couldn't surface, I was devastated. I've mourned the inability to do something that should have been so natural for me as a shifter.

All the times my grandmother watched me struggle to let my animal out surge to the forefront of my mind. The pain it caused me physically and emotionally not to be able to shift echoes through me like a fresh wound, and I realize this whole time, it's been because of the ring my gran gave me. Fury boils through my veins, and as much as I love my gran and appreciate everything she's done for me, I'm raging to know that for some reason, she lied to me.

For the first time since she died, I'm glad that she's gone. Because if I were able to confront her about this, I don't know that she and I would ever be able to come back from the fight that would take place. She's been fucking lying to me, and as soon as I can figure out how to shift out of this form and get back to that clearing and my bike, I'm going to scour Gran's house and find some fucking answers.

My wings flap and adjust my angle as I approach the lake. I have no idea how they're just doing that, but I suspect it has something to do with the hint of other consciousness I feel inside of me. I don't poke at it too much as I don't want my animal to lose focus of the awesome flying she's doing, but as soon as our four feet are planted firmly on the ground, I'll be demanding to know how the hell all of this is happening. I glide lower over the water, and my shadow flows ominously across the surface of the blue lake. I look down to search for my reflection, and shock surges through me.

I'm not a dragon, I realize, as white feathers and a black...beak? Yep, that's most definitely a beak shining back up at me from the surface of the smooth water. I have ears that are long and angle back from my face like a horse's ears do when it's angry. Large purple eyes stare back at me, the same stunned confusion swimming in them that's coursing through my insides. My wings are massive and covered in obsidian feathers that almost appear to soak up the light all around them.

The white feathers on my face continue down my neck, stopping just past my chest to make way for velvety white fur. The sun reflects off the lake, and it makes my coat shine and gleam. My arms, or front legs, are snow-feathered to the forearm, and my hands resemble a bird's feet. All five of my fingers are tipped by lethal looking black talons, but my back legs look like white furry paws, with a hint of black claws that are sheathed and waiting to be called on.

What in the flying fuck am I?

The lake ends abruptly, and I twist so that I can turn around and stare at myself some more; see what else I can find that either adds to this fucked up puzzle or helps put everything together for me. A shadow falls over me, and if I hadn't just witnessed my own shadow fall over the lake as I blocked the sun from its surface, I wouldn't know that something huge just blocked the sun above me as it flew past.

Fuck, please don't let it be a dragon!

There's a shift in the air above me, and whatever the fuck I am knows *that* is a really bad thing. I hold on for the ride as my literal fight or flight instincts take over. My wings fold in and I'm instantaneously diving through the sky. I drop like a downed plane, and if I weren't sure some big scary thing was trying to eat me right now, I'd really fucking love the speed I'm achieving. Suddenly my wings shoot out, and an updraft grabs ahold of me, redirecting my trajectory from falling to rising. I pump my powerful wings frantically, ascending, as the current helps me to move even faster. I know somehow if I can make it to the clouds, then I'll be safer, shrouded, and much harder to spot.

My speed feels supersonic, but it must not be fast enough, because just as I'm about to reach the white fluffy underbelly of the clouds, a screech-laced roar fills the air around me. The shadow attacks me from the side, and I feel like a seal that's been body slammed by a killer whale. I twist and my feet and hands dig into something hard, as I fall backwards. My own scream-screech is torn from my throat, and I rear back to avoid the black and gray beak that snaps toward my neck. Pain digs into where I'm pretty sure my stomach is, and I kick out at whatever this thing is that's hurting me.

A fluffy white furry tail—I didn't realize I had until now —cracks out and pummels the sky shadow, and I slash, kick, and hit it in an effort to get it to disengage. The ground is quickly screaming up toward us, and I can't tell if this thing is trying to rip me apart in the air or smash me to pieces against the ground. I scream again in frustration when I can't get it off of me, and we spin violently with disorienting g-force as we fall from the sky. The black-tipped beak snaps for my face again, and I manage to get a talon-capped hand up and press the attacking beak down and away from me.

Eyes the color of honey land on mine from a black feathered face, and I realize quickly that *whatever* I am, this thing is one too. I don't know what happens in that moment, but a fiery warmth roars through my body, and the sky shadow doesn't try to snap for my neck again. It almost looks... surprised.

I scream out at it in my head for it to *get off me or we're about to fucking die.*

Like it can hear me, the honey-hued eagle eyes move from mine to the threat of the rising ground at my back. The sky shadow's wings shoot out and catch the air. It releases me from its hold and—I think—tries to flip me over, but I'm falling with such force, and at such an awkward angle, that I can't get my wings out to stop myself.

The animal above me shrieks, and I can hear the panic in the sound. The next thing I know, I'm slamming into the unforgiving ground. And for the second time since I simply tried to follow my gran's wishes and spread her ashes, I feel my bones break and shatter before everything goes black.

* * *

I release a tired groan and stretch the stiffness out of my limbs. The sheets are cool against my skin, and a gentle breeze caresses my face and arms. My muscles feel tight, and I give a little screech as I flex my arms and legs and then let them relax. The sound bounces around the room and then slams back into me, bringing disjointed memories with it. I look down at my arms in awe. The last time I saw them, they were massive, muscled, feathered, and tipped with sharp ass talons. I flip my hands over, studying my limbs like somehow I'll be able to see whatever it is that I am just under my skin.

I take stock of how I feel, and I'm shocked to find that none of the overwhelming agony I felt before I passed out seems to exist anywhere in my body anymore. Nothing feels broken. I slip out of the massive bed to make sure there are no residual twinges of pain. The pale yellow sheet falls away from my body, and the cool breeze roaming all over my skin confirms that I am, without question, naked. I reach for the sheet on the bed and wrap it around me, the soft linen trailing behind me as I look over the room in search of my clothes.

The huge bed I woke up in is the only piece of furniture in here. The floor and the walls are the same soft cream color. They look like they're made out of marble, but this stone somehow looks softer. Vines have been carved into the stone at the corners of the room, and they reach up to a Gothic cathedral-style ceiling. The room is bright thanks to the massive open archways that make up the whole wall to my right. A balcony stretches out on the other side of the openings, and I'm assaulted by green trees and plants that make up the cliffside across from me.

The red-purple hued mountains I was flying through earlier flash through my mind, and I rush out onto the balcony to see if I can spot them. My heart falls when they're nowhere in sight, and I'm left even more disoriented about where I am. I turn to take in the building my balcony is attached to. The pounding sound of water surrounds me, and I stand open-mouthed and take in everything my gaze lands on. The balcony and room I'm standing in have been built into the side of a cliff. In fact, a whole *castle* seems to have been carved into the stony side of this massive mountain. There's so much intricate detail to the structure, though, that it almost looks like the cliff grew around a castle, swallowing it up and only leaving hints of it exposed to the world. A huge thundering waterfall pours off the cliff top, and I can feel some of the mist brush against me as I stand out here, exposed and reeling.

Did I die and wake up in a Lord of the Rings movie?

The distinct sound of a heavy door being opened reaches me on the balcony, and I slip behind a pillar just to my left, to hide. Boots tromp into the room, and then panicked voices float out to me.

"Where'd she go?" a masculine tenor voice asks.

Someone else groans loudly with obvious frustration. "He's going to kill us," a second, deeper voice declares, as heavy footfall quickly makes its way toward me. A man storms out to the soft looking stone banister and starts to search the sky. I take a deep, quiet inhale and catalogue his scent. I've met a plethora of different kinds of shifters in my life—wolves, pumas, even a skunk once—but I have never smelled anything like this guy.

He's huge. He's probably got a foot or more on me, and I'm six foot even. His back is broad, and tapers down nicely to a trim waist. His clothes look like they're some kind of soft gray leather that's smooth in some places and braided and more armor-like in others. It hugs his muscles and frame very closely, I observe, and then I try to shake away the heat that thought threatens to stir in me. The seam on the side of his pants and top are laced together, and the leather armor looks like it can be removed with just a couple pulls of the ties. He has two swords crossed in an *X* over his back, and the handles stick up over his shoulders.

"Cum on a tree sprite!" he shouts over the balcony. "How did the guards not see her escape? Zeph is going to gut both of us!"

He whirls around, anger dripping off of him, but before he can stomp back into the room, his dark gray eyes land on mine. They widen for a fraction of a second, and sudden heat blooms in my chest. It starts to rage like an inferno, spreading out through my limbs, and seems to get worse when he runs his warm gaze down my sheet-covered body and back up. He takes a step toward me but stops himself, shaking his head as if to clear it of something. He looks back up at me and narrows his eyes.

If Jamie Dornan and Brad Pitt were shoved into one body, it would look like this guy, well, minus the pissed off look this dude's face just morphed into. The very attractive, scruffy, and dangerous looking man shakes his head at me.

"Found her," he announces, his tone flat, his gaze now cold.

I can feel his icy assessment against my now fevered skin, and I don't know what to make of any of this. I pull the light yellow sheet tighter around my body, needing more between me and whoever this man is. *Not a man*, I tell myself as a flash of him searching through the sky streaks back through my mind. Not only does he not smell human, he was looking for something that could fly. I quickly bring my arm up to my face and smell it. The same lilac-on-a-warm-breeze scent fills my nose, and my mouth pops open, stunned. I've always smelled like wet soil and pine.

Like a wolf.

Anger bubbles inside of me, and I curse the shit out of my grandmother in my head. "Where am I?" I ask, as another person joins the guy with the angry storm clouds for eyes on the balcony.

"The Eyr—," the other guy starts to answer, but Gray Eyes gives him a glare, and he promptly shuts his mouth and drops his gaze.

"And where is that exactly?" I ask, running the half-name through my head and trying to place where the hell I am. East somewhere? I quickly dismiss that thought. These guys do not look like they're from anywhere in Asia, and I've never heard of a red-purple mountain range there—or anywhere else for that matter.

Gray Eyes scoffs. "Like we would ever tell *you* that," he declares, and then he leaves the balcony and storms back into the room. "Bring her to the Hall of Eyes. Zeph wanted to speak to her as soon as she woke up."

The now very angry, gray-eyed, broad-shouldered stranger disappears out of the room, and I stare at the now empty doorway, confused. What the hell is his problem? *I'm* the one that just woke up naked in a strange place with no idea how I got here or where here even is. If anyone should be having a tantrum, it's me.

"Yes, Altern," the light-haired man still standing across from me replies. "Come," he instructs, and then he walks away.

"Wait, where are my clothes? I can't go anywhere like this," I tell him, gesturing to the sheet wrapped around my body.

He says nothing, just walks right out the door, his back to me. I wait for a second and then decide the answers I'm looking for are probably wherever he's supposed to lead me. I let out a huff of irritation and then look down at the yellow sheet I've wrapped around me. I undo the towel tuck that's keeping the bedding on me and pull the whole thing behind me. Time to get resourceful.

I pull the sheet tight against my ass and bring the top two corners forward. I move the opening of the sheet to the side like it's supposed to be an intentional slit, and crisscross the corners of the sheet at my waist. The bed this thing fits is huge, and that works in my favor as I have plenty of fabric to cross the corners of the sheet behind my lower back, bring them forward to cross over my boobs, covering them, and then tie everything off behind my neck. I look like someone who's trying way too hard to be sexy for some frat toga party, but it will have to do.

I scramble out of the room and catch up with the none too chatty guard. I try to keep track of the empty hallways I'm led through, but it's hard to stay completely focused on that task as I try to make sure this fucking sheet doesn't fall off somehow. After maybe five minutes of winding down too many halls for me to possibly keep track of, we arrive at a pair of tall dark wood doors. There are things carved into them, but I don't get much of a chance to see what as they're flung open and I'm ushered through. I trip over some of the sheet that's pooled at my legs and feel the tie around my neck get pulled tighter. The ends don't come free, but the sheet isn't secured as tightly around my top as it was before.

The back hangs loose down my back, and my breasts are barely covered now by small ruched strips of fabric. I look like the toga edition of what not to wear, which is just perfect because, when I look up, there's a table of seven men staring at me. I recognize Gray Eyes, who is sitting to the right of a man who looks like the love-child of Kit Harington and Josh Duhamel. He's big and bulky, a touch larger than Gray Eyes but not by much. They're the biggest men I've ever seen in my life and the two largest at the table in front of me, although that's not saying much as all of the guys staring at me seem larger than the average human and much fitter at that.

My eyes roam up the muscular arms of Kit Duhamel, and I freeze when I land on his honey-hued gaze. My heart starts pounding, and an echo of the heat I just felt in my limbs back in the room with Gray Eyes warms me.

"You!" I say, and I can't tell if it's an accusation or a need for confirmation.

3

"Name and Clan?" Kit Duhamel demands, and everyone at the table glares at me even harder.

I look around the large room and try to piece together what the hell is going on. "Uhh...my name is Falon Solei Umbra," I tell them, like some nervous soldier reporting for duty. "And I'm from the um...thought-I-was-a-wolf-shifter-until-the-whole-wings-thing-happened clan." I bite down on my tongue to keep myself from rambling on about my secret-keeping bitch of a grandmother too. These guys don't look like they're messing around, and I can feel tension and menace in the air, mingling with their breezy lilac scent.

"What the rut does that mean?" Gray Eyes demands, and the hostility in the air kicks up another notch.

What the rut? I repeat in my head, trying to figure out what the fuck he just said.

"Maybe some time in the cells will strip you of your insolence," a beefy red-bearded man on the end tells me.

"You've already got my clothes, now you want my insolence, too?" I mutter to myself, but it's clear the whole table heard me. *Fuck,* Falon, *they're shifters. Every whisper around them might as well be a low key shout.* I clear my throat and look around again, like somehow answers or help are going to detach from the wall and everything will suddenly make sense. That doesn't happen, and I settle my gaze back on the table and every big ass motherfucker sitting on the other side of it.

"Before I get the whole *cell* tour, would one of you mind filling me in on what I am, where I am, and just what the hell is going on?" I ask, trying to keep my tone casual as I stomp down on the frustration brewing inside of me.

A blond guy next to Gray Eyes starts to laugh, but it's not at all friendly or bouncing with entertainment. It's cruel and resentful. My stomach flips a little, and I remind myself that as annoying as all of this is, I need to watch myself. Shifters live by a very different code than humans. Killing and fighting are commonplace, and judging by the unlit candle chandeliers above me, this place is probably working with an archaic set of rules.

"Are you really trying to convince us that you don't know what you are, let alone *who* you are or exactly where you find yourself?" the blond man questions and then punctuates it with another humorless chuckle.

"Yes..." I put my hand out and motion in the shape of a circle. "All of that, exactly."

A small rumble escapes the honey-eyed sky shadow who is now wearing a man body, and his shoulder length black curls sway as he shakes his head. "Summon Ami," he commands, and his voice sounds like the deep rumble of a volcano that's on the verge of erupting.

No one moves from the table, but I hear the door open and shut behind me as a guard from the door goes to find whoever Kit Duhamel just asked for. I stand there awkwardly, taking in the open windows and what looks to be endless blue water beyond them. I contemplate for a second diving out of them if things get too bad in here for me, but I have no idea how to make whatever I am just come out. I have zero experience with actual shifting, and I'll need to practice a shit ton before I attempt something like that. Maybe I can do that in the cells.

A growl fills the room, and I look back to find an angry honey stare fixed on me. I glare at him, not able to put my annoyance in check fast enough. I wish they'd start mumbling shit to each other so I could maybe catch a word here or there that would clue me in, but they all sit there like silent judgy fucking gargoyles.

I stare back at the light amber irises sparkling angrily at me, and it's like I suddenly feel his claws at my stomach and his hooked beak snapping at me. I breathe through the onslaught of panic that fills me as I remember falling and the feel of my animal smashing into the ground. I try to pant discreetly through the flashback, never taking my eyes off of the shifter responsible for it.

His nostrils flare slightly, and he seems almost satisfied by the anxiety he must scent in the air. That pisses me the fuck off. This asshole attacked me for no reason. He almost killed me. And now he's going to get off on my fear when he should be apologizing for what he did or explaining why he did it. Instead, he smirks at me, all high and mighty, forcing me to stand here practically naked in front of a handful of other judgmental pricks. Rage pumps through me, replacing the panic, and I welcome it.

Kit Duhamel drops his eyes from mine and dips them down my body. I can feel his warm honey-like gaze dripping down my exposed skin, and I fight a shiver of sudden need that runs up my spine. I battle the corners of my mouth as they try to tilt up in a satisfied smirk. I may not know much

22

about whatever this group of shifters is, but when it comes to the shifters I do know about, dropping your gaze while in a staring contest means submission. I don't know who honey eyes is, but he looks pretty head honcho to me.

His eyes snap up to meet mine, and the fury reflecting back at me smothers the self-satisfaction that was just floating through my chest. The doors behind me open, and I turn to see the blond guard who led me here, guiding a young man into the room. He looks like a teenager, one that's just on the cusp of puberty, and he moves to stand next to me and bows deeply at the waist in the direction of the people seated at the table.

"Yes, Syta?" he asks as he straightens up, and the honey-eyed sky shadow gives him a nod.

"Ami, please assess the proceedings from this point forward," he directs, and the Ami kid moves over to the side of the room and leans back against the wall.

I stare at him and wonder exactly what he's here to do when, out of nowhere, his brown irises and black pupils disappear, and his eyes turn entirely white.

"Holy shit," I gasp, unable to help it, and I study him even harder.

"Name and Clan?" Gray Eyes barks at me, and my curiosity flees like a bunny from a fox as I look toward the table of doom.

"Falon," I snap back, leaving my middle and last name off this time.

Movement to my right has me looking back at the white-eyed kid, and I just catch what looks like the tail end of a nod. A man with no beard and long straight brown hair knocks on the heavy table once. I'm not sure what that means, but I'm not given much time to process it before Gray Eyes is snapping at me again.

"Clan?"

I stare at his stormy gaze for a second, not sure what the hell to say. "I don't know exactly what that means, like my last name?" I inquire, uncertain. "It's Umbra. Which I already told you. If you're asking where I'm from, the answer is Colorado."

A knock raps on the table, and Gray Eyes' eyebrows drop slightly. "Colow-rah-down?" he asks, butchering the name of the state.

"Yeah, you know, America. The United States of America, to be exact," I elaborate, but he only looks more perplexed.

Another knock on the table echoes around the room, and the large bodies at the table shift with discomfort.

I can tell by all of their faces that they have no idea what I'm talking about. "What country am I in?" I ask, not able to help myself. I mean, I'm aware that Americans are known to have a bit of an ego about where we come from, but how have none of them heard of it? What kind of cut-off, hillbilly, mountain town am I in?

"You are in the Eyrie of the Hidden," the sky shadow grumbles at me, and he stares at me with a knowing look, like he expects me to recognize this place.

I quickly flick through all the world geography that I know, but nope, the Eyrie of the Hidden is not ringing any bells. "Where the hell is that?" I ask. Last I remember, I was just over the border in Alberta. Maybe this is a random Canadian town I've never heard of?

A knock slams against the table, and each of them suddenly looks as confused as I feel.

"Could that explain why she didn't carry the vow but none of us know her either?" Gray Eyes turns to his left and asks Kit Duhamel.

"Where did you find her again?" the red-bearded man on the end asks.

"The Amaranthine Mountains," Kit Duhamel mutters, and his hard stare fixes on me again, but I see a hint of curiosity in it now.

"Syta, you should never have gone out that far on your own," a dark-haired woman, who is sitting next to the blond evil laugher, speaks. I'm shocked for a minute because I thought she was a man too, but her voice is distinctly feminine even if her bulk and muscles aren't.

"That's not important," honey eyes snaps, and she immediately closes her mouth and gives an apologetic nod.

"There used to be a gate in those parts the Ouphe of old used to use," the long brown haired table knocker offers, and I realize that he's a woman too. They're both so thick and angular, I just assumed they were men, but now I'm thinking anyone with a beard or scruff is male, and anyone without facial hair might not be.

"Do you know what you are?" the blond man with the pain-promising laugh asks me.

"No," I tell him again, my own anger seeping out into the word.

I wait for the knock that proves to them I'm not lying. When it comes, they all start talking over each other in shock. I release a huff and look over at Ami. I've pieced together what he's here for, but I'm infinitely curious about how it works. Based on the state of his eyes, I'd guess it's something he can physically see. He stares at me unblinking, but the hint of a friendly smile peeks out of one corner of his mouth. I give him one back and then turn to focus on the cacophony in front of me.

"She's obviously highblood; just look at her," the blond man says.

"Maybe, but she carries no vow. Zeph confirmed it," the woman with the straight brown hair argues.

"What color was her gryphon? Maybe her natural markings mask it somehow?" the dark-haired woman counters.

"Force her to change. We can inspect her more thoroughly," someone else demands, but I'm lost to my own swirling thoughts and no longer able to track what they're saying.

Gryphon?

The name bounces around in my mind, and it conjures up images of a shit ton of English heraldry. I try to think past what I may have seen on coats of arms and connect the mythological name with what I saw in the reflection of the lake as I flew over it. Gryphons are half bird, half lion? Or maybe it can be any big cat, because the sky shadow's ass was definitely black. And mine was definitely white. I did have a tail. I remember trying to beat the shit out of Kit Duhamel, the honey-eyed sky shadow, when he attacked me. My face was very eagle like, with the exception of the long black, back-facing ears.

"Gryphon," I whisper, trying the name on to see how it feels around my body. A knowing warmth fills me, and I look down at my palms in awe.

I'm a fucking gryphon!

The air in front of me shifts, and I look up with alarm, reminded of what it felt like to get attacked in the air. Like some fucked up flashback, the sky shadow—who I'm pretty sure is the guy, Zeph, Gray Eyes was talking about—is stomping toward me, hate radiating from his eyes. I have no idea what to do. He's massive, easily seven and a half feet tall, and he looks like he wants to crush me...again.

He stops just shy of me, his chest shoving against mine slightly, and I have to fight to keep my footing and not take a step back to make room for him. I lean into him, refusing to give him my space, and my traitorous body responds to his proximity. My nipples harden against him, and just the rise and fall of his chest as he breathes, sends a zing of anticipation and pleasure straight to my clit.

"I don't know who you are, but I'm going to find out. If Lazza thinks I can be fooled by a counterfeit call and a pair of tits, he has another thing coming."

I stare up at the abhorrence pouring out of his eyes, and I bristle. I have no idea what he just said, but the tone is clear. Anger takes over, and I fist bump the death wish that just showed up inside of me. I lift my hands and push the massive fucker doing his best to intimidate me. He takes a couple steps back, and I don't know who's more shocked by that, me or him.

"Fuck you," I spit venomously at him, and the shock sluffs off his face as he charges me. He slams up against me again, and it's like he hits a barrier right where I begin. I'm ready for him this time, and I cheer loudly inside when I once again hold my ground. I'm not sure what he's going to do to me, but I know it's not going to be good. I can feel his fisted hands at his side and the rage pouring out of every pore.

He roars in my face, and I jump with surprise as the angry sound assaults me. I flinch, not able to help it, and then tense, knowing at any second the vicious sound pouring out of him will be followed by a beating. I stare at him in challenge. He's going to fucking annihilate me, but that doesn't make him the tough asshole he clearly thinks he is. He can stare into my eyes and see just how little I think of him as his fists connect with my body.

I breathe heavily, adrenaline, fear, and anger pumping through me. Shock suddenly drowns out all my other emotions as a flash of pain runs up my back. The next thing I know, a pair of large ebony-feathered wings rip out of my back. I keep my face blank in spite of what I'm feeling inside.

Well, that's fucking new.

Based on the surprised look that Zeph is now wearing, it's not only new, but apparently a pretty kick ass trick at that. I'll take it.

4

Gasps fill the room, and I whimper, wavering slightly when my wings spread to almost twice my size. They're not nearly as massive as they were when I was a gryphon though, and I wonder if they adjust in size to my different forms. Zeph stops roaring immediately, like my wings just reached out and bitch-slapped him silent. I expect the new black feathered appendages to feel heavy or force me to topple over on my back like an upturned turtle, but the opposite is true. They feel like they're a part of my body just like my arms and legs do. They feel like they've always been there and my body has always accommodated them.

Zeph's honey gaze traces the top curve of my feathers, and he rolls his shoulders as if the appearance of my wings is somehow calling to his own. The ability to partial shift is rare back in the shifter world I grew up knowing about. Judging by the reaction currently circulating through this room, I'd guess the same is true here. Zeph closes his shocked mouth, and next thing I know, he's stomping out of the room and slamming the large intricately carved doors behind him.

I turn back to the others, feeling helpless, frustrated, and fighting against the adrenaline currently slamming through my system. My stare lands on Gray Eyes' stormy gaze, and suddenly white and gray wings thrust out of his back. We both give a sharp inhale of surprise. He flexes them out behind him, his rain-cloud gray gaze never leaving mine. He gives his massive wings a quick flap, and the air stirs and whips around the room.

My wings itch to do the same thing, but I keep them tightly locked together at my back. It's clear that, for whatever reason, Zeph thinks I'm a threat despite the teenage lie detector test still leaning casually against the wall. Gray Eyes' contempt-filled stare tells me that he's feeling the same way. The last thing I need to do is get torn apart because I flapped my wings and they deciphered that as an act of aggression instead of me just stretching.

Gray Eyes pulls his wings back inside of him, and I stare at where they used to be over his shoulder. He just did that like it was as easy as breathing, and it makes envy and wonder flash through me. I take a deep breath and try to coax mine back inside, but nothing happens.

"She needs to be cleansed before we go any further," Gray Eyes declares.

The dark-haired woman gives a small nod. "Yes, Ryn. I mean, Altern," she quickly corrects when Gray Eyes—who's apparently named Ryn—narrows his eyes at her.

The way people here use Syta and Altern makes it clear that they're titles of some sort. They're said with reverence and respect and mark Zeph and Ryn as leaders or commanders maybe. It also seems anyone with a title is a raging douche bag.

"I want her doused in the tears of clarity and anything else we have that will combat any of the old magics. Let's make sure we're not up against any unforeseen variables, and then we'll see what her truth *really* looks like."

Ryn storms out, his order hanging in the air, and all but the dark-haired woman follow him. We watch each other for a moment before she steps out from behind the heavy wood table and makes her way slowly toward me. I tense as she approaches, and her critical eyes roam over every sheet clad inch of me.

"If you think I'm going to let you scrub me down, you've got another thing coming," I warn her. She just stares at me for a couple of awkward seconds before she gives me a slight nod.

"Follow me, please," she tells me, and she starts walking toward the door.

She's taller than me by probably six inches and thicker in every way. She's not as big as the males that were at the table, but she's massive by human standards. She's the biggest woman I've ever encountered, and she moves with a grace that stuns me. I can't take my eyes off of her as she practically floats over the ground. Even just her hands swaying at her sides as she walks reminds me of the time I saw this beautiful hula dance at school.

I gasp, surprised, when my wings are suddenly pulled into my back. I spin like a dog chasing its tail as I try to deduce what made them snap out and then disappear just as mysteriously. My guide doesn't even pause, and I have to shove my curiosity away and rush to catch up.

I follow her through *more* winding hallways until I find myself back in the room with the balcony and large bed that's missing a yellow sheet. She walks right past everything and through another doorway that looked like it was just part of the wall. I walk closer to where she disappeared through, wondering if it's some kind of magic, but as I get closer, I realize that the back part of the entryway blends really well and makes it look like a solid wall when it's actually recessed.

"What's your name?" I ask as I step through the hidden doorway and into a massive bathroom.

"Loa," she answers simply, not looking at me. She pulls a lever, and steaming water pours from the ceiling into a huge empty bath that's been dug into the floor of the room.

A large window-like cutout on the back wall allows natural light to illuminate the stone room, and I take it all in. Steam, and a deep musky scent I can't place, start to fill the space. It coaxes out some of the tension that's locking up my muscles, and I exhale a small sigh of relief. Loa presses another lever, but I don't notice what it does as I catch the reflection of her back in the large veined mirror she just walked in front of. She steps back to the large tub that's still filling, and I'm left staring at a shell-shocked stranger.

I know the reflection is mine because it's wrapped up in a butter-yellow sheet. It also mirrors my movements exactly when I bring my hand up and run it over my hair. I'm stunned beyond words to find that my dark brown tresses have somehow been stripped of all color. I walk closer to the mirror and reach over my shoulder to grab the tail of the tight braid I always wear when I ride my motorcycle. It's looser and a bit disheveled, but the braid is hanging in there through all the shit that's happened in the last twenty-four hours. Crap, has it even been twenty-four hours, or has it been longer? I run my fingers through the end of the braid and try to work the tangles out that are keeping it from unraveling.

What the hell?

The ends of my hair are completely white, and it darkens to the faintest of grays at my roots. I stare at the wavy kink left behind by the braid and don't even know what to think. I pull my eyes from my ghostly tresses and freeze when my gaze lands on light purple irises instead of the dark brown I've spent my life looking into. I poke at my cheek just to be sure that this is, in fact, me. The stranger in the mirror does the same. The tan skin tone I've always had is reflected back at me. My eyebrows are still dark, and long black lashes continue to frame my eyes, but my new white hair and lavender stare make me look so completely alien.

I turn to Loa. "What happened?" I ask, holding out a chunk of my now pigment challenged tresses. She looks at me like she doesn't understand the question. "My hair and eyes used to be dark like yours," I explain, but she just looks even more confused. A flash of my mother's ring, cracked and crumbling on my hand, streaks through my mind, and a growl of frustration bubbles up in my chest.

A woman walks into the bathroom at that moment and goes still. Our eyes lock onto each other in the mirror, and she stares at me open-mouthed.

"Tysa, lift your jaw off the ground and bring me the tears of clarity, verity moss, and a bottle of crushed pietersite," Loa commands.

Tysa gives a small curtsey and rushes out of the room. Loa turns back to me, and her dark judgmental gaze runs over my white hair.

"Whatever magic you were using to change your appearance must have worn off," she accuses, her nose scrunched up like she's smelled something foul.

I open my mouth to argue that it wasn't magic, but I pause. *Shit, was it magic?* Did the ring keep me from knowing what I was and also mask what I really looked like? *Have I been this purple-eyed, milky-haired, gryphon girl inside this whole time?* I've been so irritated that my gran kept all of this from me that I haven't spent much time focusing on the why of it all. I turn away from Loa and take in my reflection again. My coloring is incredibly unusual, and I would have stuck out like a sore thumb back home.

Loa indicates that the bath is ready, and I untie the sheet corners from around my neck and step out of the fabric. Lost in my efforts to try and piece things together, I sift through my thoughts as I step down into the bath. My skin stings when it comes into contact with the hot water, but I ignore it and step all the way in until it laps just below my breasts. There's a shelf built into the side where I can sit, and I plop down absently as I run through everything I thought I knew about my mother, father, and grandmother.

A hand grips the wet hair hanging on my back, and I flinch away from the touch. Loa narrows her eyes at me, and I mirror her irritated expression.

"I was ordered to cleanse you," she tells me, like that solves any issues I might have with her touching me.

"I can *cleanse* myself," I counter, taking another step further out of her reach.

"That's not how this works. We need to ensure you're free of any illusions or magic."

"By what, scrubbing my ass crack and armpits?" I interject. "Not a chance in hell that's happening."

Loa's face mottles with anger. "Listen, you highborn little chit, you may be used to getting your way where you come from, but you *are* a prisoner here. You *will* do as you're told, or your time here will become significantly more uncomfortable. We will not risk the safety of the entire pride because you have delicate sensibilities."

Tysa strolls through the entrance to the bathroom, carrying everything she was instructed to get. She cringes as she walks into the thick tension in the room. Loa snaps her fingers at me and points to the space in the water directly in front of her. She doesn't say anything, but the command is clear. Since I'm not a puppy, I stay exactly where I am in the water. If she wants to cleanse me, she can bring her thick-ass in here and try it. This tub is plenty big enough to drown her in. I mentally snort at that thought. She's massive and cut like a fucking boulder; I'm pretty sure if a drowning takes place in this bathtub, it will be mine not hers.

We shoot eye daggers at each other for a beat, neither of us giving an inch.

"Tysa, go collect some guards. It seems our guest prefers things done the hard way."

Tysa sets everything down on a counter housing a wash basin and hurries back out of the room. I have to visibly work to not cringe at Loa's *hard way* statement. Having this bitch rub all over me is bad enough, but now I need to have some fucking guards thrown into the mix, too? I bite down on the *wait* that sits on my tongue. *I can't back down*, I tell myself. She's just another shifter. Yes, she happens to be a big scary half bird, half lion or something else, but a shifter is a shifter. And if you want to get anywhere and earn any modicum of respect from a shifter, you have to back up the dumbass things that come out of your mouth.

Stupid mouth and stupid fucking pride. And fuck these stupid assholes and their cleansing bullshit.

I shake out the unease that crashes through me and try to look as tough and kickass as I can. Screw this bossy bitch. Zeph attacked *me*. He smashed *me* into the ground and then brought me here. I woke up without any clothes and put up with their unwarranted hostility. I answered all of their questions honestly—even the white-eyed kid told them as much—and now they want to humiliate me even more with this shit. The *hard way*, it is.

Adrenaline pumps through me, and a tremor starts in my hands from it. I feel light and shaky, and try to mentally prepare for whatever is about to go down. Loa has a glint of amusement in her eyes, and I debate if I can make it disappear by splashing hot water at her. The sound of heavy footfall reaches me in the tub and echoes in the bathroom. The thunderous stomping is almost perfectly synchronized with the hammering beat of my heart. The acoustics in the bathroom make it impossible to discern how many guards are about to march through the doorway, and I sink lower into the steaming water and ball my fists with anticipation.

Tysa has a sheepish look on her face when she rounds the corner and steps lightly into the room. I get my *don't fuck with me* glare set in place, but it cracks when Ryn rounds the corner behind Tysa, no other guards on his heels.

"Can I help you, Altern?" Loa asks, flustered by his sudden appearance.

"I was told you needed assistance," he retorts, his deep voice bouncing around the stone bathroom and his eyes finding mine.

"My apologies, Altern," Loa tells him, and the scathing look she shoots Tysa could melt steel. "Tysa was supposed to fetch guards. This is nothing you need to worry about."

"I'm here now, so what seems to be the problem?" he barks, and Loa shoots Tysa another withering glare.

"She refuses to be cleansed," Loa finally tells him after a hesitant beat.

"No, I refuse to let you touch me," I clarify. "I'll rub whatever you want on my own body; I don't need some bitch I don't know doing it."

Ryn watches me for a moment and then starts to undo the ties of his armor.

"Altern?" Loa inquires, and my heart rate kicks up even more.

Ryn shoots an irritated look at Loa. "You said you needed help, so I'll hold her."

"Altern, this is a job for the guards, not you. I'm sure you have far more important things to—"

Ryn silences her with a look, pulls his armored vest off and starts on the ties of his undershirt. Something akin to excitement lights up inside of me, and I study the unexpected feeling for a second. He's going to get into this bath with me and hold me down while they scrub me clean with moss and pour potions on me, from the look of things. Why the fuck does his presence in this fucked up situation now excite me? I shake off the sudden onslaught of giddiness which must be a clear indication of the mental breakdown I'm suffering from, probably due to all of the shock that's recently sucker punched me, and look around the room with panic. I don't know what the hell is going on, but I need to get the fuck out of here.

I scramble to the back of the tub and push myself up and over the rim. Water splashes around me as I rush to get on my feet, and when I spin around, Loa is on one side of the in-ground tub and Ryn is on the other. They're blocking my escape routes, and I back up to get as far away from them as I can. Loa's eyes narrow at me, but Ryn seems to be tracking the water that's dripping down my naked body. His pupils dilate as he runs his gaze down and slowly back up. His Adam's apple bobs as he swallows, and when his gray eyes find mine again, there's surprising heat in his gaze.

My back hits the sill of the window behind me, and a breeze rushes in from outside. White strands of hair snake in and out of my line of sight, but I don't take my eyes off of my captors. I place my hand on the edge of the open window, and a deep rumbling sound fills the bathroom. Ryn's eyes morph from molten to warning, and embarrassingly my body responds to his growl. My nipples harden, and a fluttering sensation works its way down my abdomen and settles between my thighs. Need pools inside of me, and the idea of Ryn having his hands all over me suddenly feels like a really fucking good idea.

My fingers dig into the stone surrounding the opening behind me, and I momentarily snap myself out of my lecherous thoughts. *What in the fuck is going on with me?* I've been kidnapped, held against my will, and now they're threatening to assault me. But apparently, *my* fucked up brain is cool with it as long as the one doing the assaulting is this hot as fuck Ryn asshole? Have I been drugged? I quickly look from Ryn to Loa, ensuring she's still well out of reaching distance, and then I turn and dive out of the window.

So much for practicing a lot before doing this. Here's to hoping I can shift and save my ass, otherwise this is going to fucking hurt.

5

Ryn bellows a "noooo," but it's quickly lost in the loud sound of whooshing air as it streaks past me. I swallow the terror that my free fall sends coursing through me and reach into where my gryphon is evidently having a nap. I have no fucking clue how to wake her up, and it's starting to get easier to make out the details below me. A shadow falls over me, and I know exactly what that means. Like I'm swimming through water and not plummeting to a very painful crush injury, I use my hands and legs to flip myself over.

A furious looking Ryn, who clearly has no trouble getting his wings to cooperate, shoots straight toward me as fast as a bullet. A tingling runs up my back, and when it gets to my shoulder blades, huge black wings shoot out of me. Just fucking great; it seems they only want to come out and play in the vicinity of very hot assholes. The sudden appearance of my new feathered ebony appendages puts me into a spin in the air, and I try to fan out my wings as much as possible to stop the tornado-like momentum.

Ryn crashes into me and wraps his huge arms around my waist to stop me from spinning. I'm slammed back, but he holds me tightly against him, his grip vice-like as his huge gray and white wings shoot out to slow us down. An ache starts in my stomach, and I feel the drive to wrap my naked body around him and hold on tightly. So instead, I punch him in the face.

He grunts and then roars at me in frustration, and the angry sound shoots right to my clit. Clearly something inside of me is broken, and I ignore its cuddly prompts as I scratch and scramble to get out of Ryn's embrace. I knee him in the stomach in a last ditch effort, and his grip loosens just enough that I can get my legs up between us and kick off of his rock hard abs to get away. I have just enough time to flip around and get my wings spread out to try and slow myself as much as possible before I slam into what I'm pretty sure is a fruit stall.

I cover my face with my hands and scream as wood splinters all around me, and the sound of fabric tearing fills my ears. Something smashes into my left wing, and I grunt from the pain and try to pull them tight against my back to protect them. I jerk to a stop suddenly, my leg caught on something, and I clench my teeth against the pain that shoots up my thigh. Something wet and sticky covers my skin, and I glance down, worried it's blood. A light pinkish juice covers my torso and chest, and I look over and deduce it's from the yellow fruit I just pulverized.

I groan and take stock of myself. Bruised but not broken, it seems, and I sit up and unwrap some dark blue fabric from around my leg. It looks like it used to be part of the canopy of the stall I just crashed through, and I pull at it until it rips all the way free. I brush shards of wood from my arms and legs and wrap the canopy fabric around me and tie it off. My body protests as I stand up. The fabric of the canopy I'm now wearing is short but thankfully covers all of my personal bits. I snap my wings out behind me, shaking them free of debris, and breathe a sigh of relief as they seem to be fine. There would be no escaping with a broken wing.

Shrill screams and hurried shouts break through my collision-induced fog, and I look up to find I've just crash-landed into some kind of marketplace. I'm surrounded by other wooden stalls that are housing food, fabric, jewelry and far too many stunned faces staring back at me. I scan my surroundings and see a group of people huddling around something. Part of a gray-tipped white wing is visible on the ground, and I realize they're surrounding Ryn. I feel the urge to check on him, and a twinge of guilt shoots through me at the thought that he might be hurt.

I take a step toward the gathering crowd, but a man moves to get in my way protectively. The stranger's block snaps me from my empathetic thoughts, and I start to back up and look around for an escape.

We're in a packed dirt clearing, surrounded by houses with a tall cliff on one side and a forest on the other. I bolt past the wreckage I just caused and snake between a pair of houses. Shouts to stop sound off behind me, but I push my legs faster, hoping I can make it to the trees about twenty feet away. I don't know why I feel like once I'm in the trees, I'm safe. I have no clue where I am or where I'm running to. These shifters acted like they'd never heard of America, and they said shit about a gate and something about Ouphe—whatever the fuck that is—so I don't even know if I'm on the same planet anymore.

The trees look to be some kind of massive ancestor of a pine. I've never seen the redwood trees in California, but my imagination tells me these could probably be dead ringers. I'm panting and working hard to pull oxygen into my lungs, and I debate trying to hide behind a huge trunk and catch my breath and bearings for a minute. I don't hear or see anyone following me, and I wonder if they were in too much shock. If they were, it probably won't last long, so I push myself to keep moving.

Twigs, rocks, and other sharp things dig into my feet, and I wince with every footfall. My eyes bounce around my surroundings while simultaneously trying to pick the least painful path through the trees. My body feels run down and hollow, and I thank the adrenaline and fear still pumping through me, as that's all I am currently running on. I try to pull my wings back in, but they won't listen. I debate climbing to the top of a tree and trying to fly away, but I figure I'm harder to find here amidst the trees than I would be in the sky.

I step on another rock and bite back the yelp that wants to escape. Tears well up in my eyes, and I can't help but chuckle humorlessly at their appearance. *I crash into a makeshift building and brush it off, but a rock sets me over the edge?* I look around and try to find a safe space to stop and catch my breath. I need to come up with a better plan than run and hope they don't catch me. I look up into the insanely tall trees and decide I'd probably be safest up in the branches. The lowest offshoots from the trunk are easily fifteen feet above my head, and I ponder for a minute how the hell I'm going to get up there.

I mentally slam a palm against my forehead when I remember I have wings. *Fucking hell, Falon, get it together.* I spread out my ebony additions and give a couple test flaps. I crouch a little and then pump them harder, and I have to work hard to keep from whooping in triumph when I'm lifted off the ground and up into the air. I fly like a drunk pigeon but manage to get myself perched on some branches about thirty feet off the ground. By the time I get myself snuggled safely against the trunk and get enough fabric from my canopy dress under my ass to keep it from chaffing, I'm ready to have a serious heart to heart with my gryphon.

I don't know where the hell she went, but we need to come to some kind of an understanding. She very clearly knows what she's doing when I'm shifted and she's in control. I didn't have any issues with flying as a gryphon— well, not up until the sky shadow attacked us. I need to work hardcore on calling her or connecting or whatever the hell I need to do to master my shifts and winged abilities, because we need to get the hell out of here, and it's not going to happen without my gryphon stepping up and showing me how to get shit done.

I sag against the tree trunk, the reddish-brown bark digging into my back, and rub my feet. Gradually my labored breathing slows, proof that I need to up my cardio game. The fight or flight that's been hammering through my veins slowly fades, and with it goes any desire to move from this spot. I'm shrouded by clumps of pine needles the size of my forearm, and I feel hidden and protected. Logically I know I haven't put enough distance between myself and my captors, and I know with every second I sit up here, they're probably closing in. Which means I need to move, but I'm struggling to convince my exhausted body of that.

The sun sinks closer to the horizon, and the shadows in the forest wake up and stretch. I wrap my wings around me and breathe my warm breath into the cocoon I've made around myself. The temperature is gradually dropping— with the right clothing and gear, it'd be perfect camping weather—however, I'm one ripped up piece of canopy away from being naked, and the cooling air bites at my skin in warning.

Reluctantly I admit to myself that I need to find someplace warmer because this tree limb is not going to cut it for the night. Slowly I stand up, and my stiff muscles protest against the movement. I'm on the verge of unfurling my wings and figuring out how to fly down from this tree, when voices and footfall reach me. I go still.

I focus and try to listen past the sudden hammering of my heartbeat in my ears. They sound like they're getting closer, and I'm not sure if I can outrun them. I inch closer to the tree trunk and bring my wings up to block me as much as possible. If they don't look up, I'll be fine. The voices grow louder. It's definitely more than one person, but I have no idea how many. I'm tempted to shut my eyes and hope the *if I can't see you, you can't see me* theory works in this case, but I can't seem to look away from the ground directly below my hiding spot.

Panic races through me as Ryn and a handful of other guards come into view, but it's challenged by the sudden relief that tries to take over. I swat that emotion away. I shouldn't care if the bossy gryphon shifter is okay. The longer he would've stayed out of commission from our crash, the better chance I would have of getting the hell away from here—wherever here is anyway. I don't know if it's empathy or my own shifter side pushing me to have the feels for these captor assholes, but I feel like I'm fighting them and myself, and it's weird as fuck. I'm typically one to follow my instincts, but right now my instincts and my brain are at war, and I'm struggling to sort through the mess of emotions.

The guards are scanning the ground, looking for tracks, I realize. Ryn stops just past the base of my tree and bends over to pick something up. He looks around the ground and then slowly stands. *Don't look up. Don't look up,* I chant in my head on a loop as if it will somehow keep any of them from doing exactly that. I squint to try and see what Ryn now has gripped in his fist. I pale when I make out the black feather he's now gripping.

"She definitely came this way, but it looks like she took

to the sky here," he announces, and then every one of them looks up.

Shit. Shit, shit! I internally scream and do my best to think invisible thoughts. The three seconds that they spend peering up past the trees feels like hours, and I'm terrified someone is going to hear the slamming of my heart against my sternum.

"Call off the ground search. We'll double the air sentries. She won't get far even with the storm rolling in to give her cover," Ryn orders, and all but one of the guards turns around and heads back the way they came. The guard that didn't move starts to look through the trees more carefully, and I know it's only a matter of time before his hawk eyes land on me. I work to slow my panic-laced breathing and hope somehow I can outsmart or outfly the last remaining guard and Ryn. I stop myself from looking up to gauge how far I need to get before I hit treetop-free sky, knowing if I move even slightly, I might give myself away.

Ryn mumbles something to the guard, but I can't make out what it is. A couple beats later, the guard stops his scanning of the massive trees around him and salutes Ryn before marching away. Ryn stands exactly where he is and scours the ground around him again. He pulls the charcoal-colored feather that clearly fell from one of my wings, through the palm of his other hand absently as he searches the ground for something. Each stroke of my abandoned feather through his strong fist sends a shiver higher and higher up my spine. It's like I can feel the soft touch up my naked back and across the tops of my wings.

A slow heat starts to unfurl in me, and my brain and body start to war again. I want to jump down and replace the ghost of his touch with the real thing, and yet I know in my mind, that's a dumb fucking thing to do. I bite the inside of my cheek and watch him crack his neck from side to side.

He brings the feather up to his nose and pulls in a deep inhale. I can picture his dark gray eyes scanning everything around him, and I'm actively fighting against the part of me that wants him to look up and spot me.

Ryn tucks my feather inside the waist of his pants. I trace his shirtless torso with my eyes, caressing the dips and peaks of his muscles as he turns to follow the direction the guards disappeared in. Loss blooms inside of my traitorous body, and I hold in the relieved exhale that wants to escape out of my lips. I stand frozen against the tree trunk for probably way longer than necessary, but I can't bring myself to move too soon. The thought that somehow this is all a trap keeps flashing like a warning in my mind, and I worry that as soon as I jump down, I'll be pounced on by a bunch of guards.

I listen closely to the sounds of this strange forest all around me, but I don't hear or see anything that makes me think my paranoia is justified. The sun drops even more, and the growing chill in the air finally spurs me into action. I step away from my hiding spot and scan the forest floor one more time before spreading my wings and jumping off the thirty-foot-high branch I'm standing on. My wings slow my rapid descent a little, and a surprised noise sneaks out of me when I land on my feet. This agile, land-like-a-cat thing is new, but I push past my awe and focus on what's around me. I fold my wings back behind me and wait for any hint of a trap to reveal itself.

When nothing moves toward me and no new sounds of pursuit reach my ears, I sprint in the opposite direction Ryn and his guards went. I wince at my sore feet and slow a little, trying to pick my path better. I can't afford to get hurt because I'm rushing, and I decide a steady brisk pace is probably smarter. I make sure to stick close to the massive trees surrounding me so the sentries in the sky can't spot me easily. My body is sticky and gross from the residue of whatever fruit juice I got myself coated in when I crashed into the fruit stall, and my makeshift dress keeps trying to fall off.

I stop to tie it more securely, and I notice the faint sound of rushing water in the distance. My mouth goes even drier, and my body makes its demand for hydration known. Apparently, just the thought of water has my body moving toward it. I tie the too short, inadequate dress tighter around me and quietly make my way toward what sounds like a waterfall. I try to be as alert of my surroundings as I can be. So far I haven't run into any scary animals, but I'm all too aware that I have no idea what exists in this forest. I weave between house-sized tree trunks, whose branches and needles hide me from the sky, until I reach the end of the tree line.

I stare out between two massive tree trunks at a small waterfall that feeds a daintily flowing stream. Steam rises off of the water, and that same unfamiliar musky scent the water in the bathroom had drifts over to where I'm standing, studying the foreign terrain. It must be some kind of hot spring, which explains where the warm water for my bath came from. Oddly, this water lacks the telltale sulfuric odor that the hot springs back home always seem to have. There's a collection of small pools on either side of the narrow river, and I stare at them longingly. This isn't the cool stream I was hoping for, but the steam rising off of this water beckons me all the same.

Warmth laps at my hiding spot, and my skin prickles, caught between the promised heat of the water and the cooling air of the night. The forest has welcomed dusk into its embrace, and the shadows stretch out, eager for the night. The light around me is fading fast, and everything is cloaked in the promise of more darkness with each passing minute. The sound of water plummeting from the small cliff above me fills my ears, and I slowly start to put together a plan. I can wash off, warm up, and either climb up into a tree and rest as much as I can for the night, or I can work on my shifting. If I can coax my gryphon into cooperation, then maybe we can make a break for it under the shroud of night.

An image of my reflection bouncing back up at me as I flew over the lake creeps into my mind. I recall that, even though my wings are black as night, the rest of my gryphon form is white. I huff out the worry that bubbles up inside of me with that realization. Ryn said there was a storm coming, maybe my gryphon knows how to be stealthy as fuck, or better yet, maybe she can kick some serious ass and fight her way out of here if she needs to. I try not to roll my eyes at that thought. I remind myself that when Zeph attacked after my first shift, my gryphon and I didn't go down without a fight. *We held our own pretty well*, I tell myself, and I stand a little taller and embrace the macho *I got this* feeling as it rears up inside of me.

I step slowly away from the trees, painfully aware of how exposed I suddenly am. There's no canopy of branches, needles, and leaves to hide me away, and I suddenly feel hunted. The *I got this* attitude I was just wrapping around myself tries to make a break for it, but I reach out and snatch it back. I apply a solid stranglehold around the faux reassurance, and chant a *fake it till you make it* mantra until I'm standing at the lip of a steaming pool of amazing smelling water.

The hot spring is about the size of an above ground pool the neighbors down the road used to let the neighborhood kids play in every summer when I was growing up. Thankfully, I can see through the water to the bottom, and relief fills me when nothing creepy is swimming around in it and it doesn't look very deep. There's no sign of boiling or anything else that would hint that this water is dangerous, so I hold my breath and dip the tip of my dirt crusted foot in it. I exhale the tension holding my body hostage when my foot doesn't melt off and nothing slithers out of the surrounding rocks to try and eat me.

My foot stings a little from the heat, but I dip it further in; I can't waste too much time out here in the open. I look around me and up at the sky again to make sure I haven't been spotted, and then I untie the knot holding the canopy fabric around me and set the dark blue bundle on a rock just to my right. It has some fruit juice residue on the side that met my skin, but I can flip it around and use it to dry off and wear when I'm done. I slip into the warm water and hiss as the stinging sensation I felt on my foot lights up all over my now mostly submerged body.

The water is just a little too hot for my cold skin, but I know I'll adjust in a couple of minutes. I swim out, away from the edge at my back, and find I can't touch the bottom of the pool. I tread water and stare at the ripples all around me, making sure I'm still safe and alone. I quickly wash the sticky layer of dried fruit juice from my skin, and my gaze flits from the water to the surrounding forest, up to the sky, and back again as I do. The warm water suddenly feels amazing, and it's very tempting to just sit here and prune out, but I'm too exposed. I twist back and forth in the water, hoping the agitation is enough to get my wings clean.

I take a deep breath and drop under the warm water, scrubbing the sticky out of my tangled hair. My feet touch the bottom of the pool, and I realize it's about six inches deeper than I am tall. White strands of my hair float around me, and I run my fingers through it and try to get it as clean as possible. My lungs start to burn with the need for oxygen, and I slowly surface and swim for the rock that I left my towel-dress-combo on.

Time to move onto phase two of my escape-and-evade

plan. I freeze in the water when I realize that my towel dress is no longer crumpled on the rock where I left it.

"Looking for this?" a deep voice questions, and I whirl around in the water to find Ryn standing on the other side of the pool, holding my tattered piece of blue canopy.

Adrenaline hammers through me as his stormy gray eyes meet mine in challenge. I can practically hear him encouraging me to just try to run. I say nothing as I attempt to quickly come up with a plan to get out of the water and away from him as quickly as possible, which is probably delusional, wishful thinking, but that doesn't mean I'm not going to try.

6

Ryn is fully dressed now. He has a fawn-colored shirt under his gray leather armor. The swords he had crossed at his back are missing, and he's holding a brown leather bag in the hand that's not fisted in my makeshift dress. I ignore my body's response to him, and as soon as my back hits the edge of the pool, I reach back and push myself out of the water. I don't take my eyes from Ryn, but his steel-coated gaze drops down my body like it did in the bathroom. I start to back away, hoping somehow that he'll be so distracted by my hardening nipples he won't notice I've made it to the tree line where I can try to make a run for it.

Surprisingly, my plan seems to work. Ryn doesn't make a move for me as I steadily back away from him. He's transfixed, not even muttering a sound of warning or disagreement as I calmly inch closer to escape. Ryn's gaze meets mine just as I slam into something large and unmovable behind me. I know I'm nowhere near the tree line, and judging by the nonplussed look on Ryn's face, he's either unconcerned by whoever I just walked into, or doesn't care if I'm about to get eaten by something.

"Did you get everything we need?" Zeph's deep voice rumbles behind me, the vibration of it moving from his chest into my wings where they're pressed against him.

I take a stride forward in an effort to sprint away from the mountain of a shifter at my back, but he reaches out and grabs me by the nape of my neck, like some naughty kitten, and pulls me back into him. I growl my displeasure at being manhandled, but I'm no match for either of these guys, and we all know it. I search the depths of my soul, shouting for my bitch of a gryphon to wake the fuck up and help a girl out, but all I manage to rouse is a satisfied warm feeling that crawls through me as Zeph and Ryn talk with each other.

If it wasn't for the wings that I can't seem to put away, I'd wonder if I was in fact still a latent. Maybe I just imagined myself as a gryphon, because I sure as fuck can't get her to work with me when I'm clearly in a state of crisis.

I never did like fucking birds.

Not even my attempt to piss my animal off results in anything, and I check back into the here and now, where I'm being held against a strong body and doing my best not to like it.

"What are you guys going to do?" I ask, as I watch Ryn kneel down and start to pull things out of the brown leather bag he's clutching. I ignore the ring of excitement I can hear in my voice and immediately question whether Stockholm syndrome kicks in *this* fast?

"We're going to finish what you tried to stop in the bathroom," Ryn tells me as he pulls out the same items that Tysa had clutched in her arms.

I expect Loa—and the guards she threatened would hold me down—to come stomping out of the forest, but to my surprise, it doesn't happen. I squirm to get out of Zeph's hold, but he just grips my neck tighter. His domination stirs something inside of me, and at first I'm not sure what it is. My vision sharpens, and a prickle moves through me, and I immediately recognize the signs my grandmother used to tell me about *the shift*. The feathers on my wings ruffle and fluff up, and I welcome the stubborn bitch of a gryphon inside of me to wake the fuck up and take over.

Finally!

Ryn's head snaps up from where he's arranging all the vials and bowls on a rock. "She's waking," he announces, his tone laced with warning.

"I know, I can feel it," Zeph tells him.

"Well, if you don't want to—"

I don't hear the rest of what Ryn has to say, because the next thing I know, Zeph is leaning over me, and his lips are inches away from the shell of my ear.

"Shhhh," he soothes. "I've got you now, little sparrow, no one is here to hurt you. You're safe in our hands," he reassures, and just like that, I can feel my gryphon sinking away.

"No," I yell in objection, and I start to work harder to try and get away from Zeph. *We are not okay; do you not see that I'm naked and being manhandled? We're about as far from being okay as it fucking gets! Where are you going?* I scream at my gryphon, but she disappears all the same.

I try to stretch out my wings to break Zeph's hold and wiggle away, but he just pins me tighter to him. My gryphon doesn't respond to anything that's happening to me this time, and impotent frustration barrels through me. I kick, claw and punch at anything I can, but Zeph just chuckles in my ear, pissing me off even more. I grit my teeth and screech out my anger. I pull a solid bitch move and grab a fist full of his black wavy locks and yank hard.

Zeph bites me.

Not hard enough to draw blood, but he chomps down on where my neck meets my shoulder and applies pressure until his meaning is clear. He's seen my bitch move and raised me a bitch move.

I let go of his hair, and he releases his teeth from my neck. He starts to frog-march me back to the water's edge, his big body herding me exactly where he wants me to go. I pretend the goose bumps that rise all over my body are from the cold and not in any response to his dominant behavior. I've always liked some *fight* in my partners, but I've never experienced anything like this before. In the past, I've always ended up being the dominant person in my relationships, and as much as I've fantasized about finding a big alpha asshole, now that one is holding me by the nape and marching me somewhere I don't want to go, I can't say I'm a huge fan of it.

"Don't move," Zeph warns me when we get to the rocky lip of the pool I was cleaning up in previously, and his grip loosens from my nape.

I immediately dash to the right, but Zeph reaches out and plucks me back to where he wants me. We repeat this a couple more times before I accept that I'm not getting away. I stare daggers at him as he reaches down and starts to unlace the black leather armor he's wearing. I can't seem to look away as he unties his vest on one side and then slips it and the black undershirt off. I take in all seven plus feet of him, every inch hard muscle covered in soft olive-toned skin, dusted with black hair on his chest, arms, and the happy trail that leads into his pants. He reaches down and starts to undo the laces at his crotch, and my fascination turns into panic.

A weird keening sound escapes me as terror bubbles up my throat. My wings seem to spring into action of their own accord and start to flap furiously in an effort to get me the fuck out of here. Zeph's honey-dipped gaze snaps up to mine, and his eyes widen at the fear he must see there. He takes a step toward me as I lift off of the ground, but arms wrap around me from behind, and I scream and thrash to get out of Ryn's hold.

"You're okay," he tells me over and over again. I fucking hate that tears start to stream down my cheeks as I rage and swear and fight as hard as I can to get away. My gryphon doesn't even stir, and I curse her and them and my grandmother for getting me into this situation. I've never felt so fucking helpless in my life, and if I make it out of this alive, I will do everything I can to never feel this way again.

"I will fucking die before I let you rape me," I screech at them, and I slam my head back, hoping it connects with Ryn's face somehow and breaks something, but the fucker is too tall, and all I manage to slam into is his muscled chest.

Zeph freezes, and his eyes flash with something as a growl slips out of his mouth. "We would never dishonor a woman or ourselves in that way," he tells me, and I think I catch a flicker of hurt in his eyes before indignation snuffs it out.

"Then what the fuck are you doing?" I ask, confused, my eyes dipping to the untied laces of his pants.

"We have to cleanse you," Ryn tells me, and his hold on me loosens ever so slightly.

"Yeah, you keep saying that, but what the fuck does that *mean*?" I demand.

"We have to make sure you're not here to hurt us or the pride. We can only confirm that by making sure you and the truth aren't cloaked in magic somehow," Zeph tells me, his voice a deep rumble. "Every inch of you will be washed with the tears of clarity, and then you'll be scrubbed clean with verity moss. Once that's been done, you will take a tincture made from axiom leaf. We will question you again, and then the truth in what you're saying will be certain and unquestionable," he tells me as if it's all so simple.

I picture his hands on my body as he works to rid me of magic I don't even have, and heat flutters through my stomach. "Fine," I tell him, and Zeph's mouth hangs open for a second in surprise. "I'll bathe in whatever you want, but I can do it myself. I don't want either of you touching me."

"It doesn't work that way," Ryn starts to say, but I cut him off.

"Then you *do* dishonor me," I accuse, using the term that Zeph did and trying to ignore the fact that I sound like the dragon from Mulan.

Zeph growls and steps into me, pressing me deliciously between him and Ryn. "I will not risk the lives of many for the discomfort of one," he snarls at me. "This is a necessity, not an act of gratification," he declares, and the look he gives me as he does has me feeling like a bug he'd rather crush under his shoe than touch.

I look away from the scathing judgement in his eyes. "And when this is done, I can go home?" I ask, my voice small as the fight in me slowly drifts away.

"We'll do what we can, yes," Ryn tells me, and he drops his strong arms from my body.

I don't miss the fact that what he just said wasn't actually a *yes*, but I don't challenge it. "Fine," I consent, and I side step out of the gryphon sandwich I'm currently liking way too much. I spread my arms out in invitation and wait for them to do whatever they need to do.

Zeph gives a slight nod to Ryn, who picks up a glass bottle of clear liquid. He grabs the now empty brown leather bag that he brought everything in and bends over to fill it with warm water from the pool. He hands the waterskin to Zeph who grabs it and holds it in front of Ryn. Ryn pours some of the clear liquid into the pouch of steaming water, and Zeph cinches the top with a meaty hand and shakes the water inside.

"Tip your head back," Zeph orders me, but I just stare at him unmoving.

"We will start with your hair, then your face, arms, torso, hips, legs, and lastly your feet," he informs me, and I swear his voice gets deeper with each listed part of my body.

I do as I'm told, and as soon as my face is turned up to the sky, Zeph pours the contents of the skin slowly and carefully through my hair. I gasp in surprise when Ryn's fingers comb through my locks, and he works the tears-of-clarity-laced water into my scalp like an award winning head masseuse. I have to actively battle against the satisfied groan that tries to sneak out of me as Zeph pours warm water on my head and Ryn's magic fingers go to work. It's over before I want it to be, and I try to mask my humph of disapproval with a cough.

The waterskin is refilled and mixed, and I hold my breath as it's poured over my face, neck and chest. My eyes snap open, and I freeze when Ryn reaches around me from behind and cups the bottoms of my breasts ensuring water makes its way under them. It's clear they have a no-nook-or-cranny-left-untouched policy at work, and my heart picks up as water is poured on me and Ryn's hands move down my body. I should *not* be fucking enjoying this, but there's no hiding the truth from myself, because for whatever reason, I really fucking am.

I put full blame on my bitch of a gryphon who is apparently pumping some baser animal need through me to combat the good sense I was born with. She may be all for this alpha *do what I say* bullshit, but I don't want to be. Usually I can count on a little sharp wit coupled with a venomous retort to get me out of most sticky situations. But mouthing off gets me nowhere here. They're bigger and stronger than I am, and they have the added bonus of knowing where the fuck they are.

Ryn's hands move down to my hips, and he brings them in to skim my lower abdomen. Lust and alarm war inside of me, and I step back from his touch.

"I will *cleanse* that myself, asshole, thank you very much," I snap at him with a glare. I reach my hands out and cup my palms together and wait for Zeph to pour the water in my bowled palms. I stand like that for a couple beats, waiting to see if they'll argue, but as warm water fills my hands, relief washes through me.

I splash water between my thighs dampening the now dry curls there. I've never been self-conscious of my body. Growing up around shifters, nudity is common place and not at all taboo or socially unacceptable. But right now in this moment, with these two watching my every move, their hands and gazes running over my naked body, I feel more vulnerable than I ever have in my life. A shiver runs up my back. The cool night air works to steal the warmth of the water from my body, and I'm filled with conflicting emotions.

The skin is filled up and mixed one last time, and Ryn and Zeph make quick work of my legs and feet. Ryn acts like we're done, and I open my mouth to ask about my wings. *It has everything to do with not wanting to repeat this whole forced bathing situation and nothing to do with the desire to have his hands on me again*, I tell myself adamantly...multiple times. Zeph presses his hand at the base of my spine, and he slowly traces up my vertebrae, stopping at the base of my wings. He applies a slight pressure between my shoulder blades, and a moan forms in my throat at the tingling sensation his touch starts in my back. My wings make a snapping noise, and then all of a sudden, the weight of them is gone from my back and shoulders.

I spin like a dog chasing its tail, looking over my

shoulder to confirm that they're gone. I look up at Zeph, shocked. "How did you do that?" I ask in awe.

He just glares at me with obvious disdain, and I try not to shrink under his hateful gaze. *What the fuck is that for?*

"In the water," Ryn commands.

He moves away from me to grab a handful of the moss he set on a rock by the pool, and I pull my gaze away from Zeph's loathsome stare and watch Ryn. I suddenly realize that I'm transfixed and practically drooling over his ass as he bends over, and I quickly tear my eyes away from his glutes and look out toward the trees with intense longing. A deep growl starts next to me, and Zeph makes his warning clear. I turn to meet his eyes again, the *fuck you* clear in my gaze and square off with him for a minute.

I tell myself to *just get this over with*. Once they know I'm telling the truth, I can go home and all of this will just be some confusing jumble of hot-as-fuck-fantasy mixed with confusing nightmare. I narrow my eyes at Zeph and move past him to step back into the pool. I would go for the aggressive shoulder slam as I walk past him, but I'm pretty sure that would do more damage to me than it ever would to his gargantuan ass.

The water once again stings my skin, too warm for my cold, numb limbs, but I grit my teeth against it and look up just in time to see Zeph untying the strings of his pants.

"Those will stay on," I growl at him, and he looks from me to the water, down to his pants like I'm crazy for suggesting such a thing. "It's bad enough that you're putting me through all this, but I refuse to be in here with either one of you naked," I demand.

"We won't hurt you," Ryn defends, and I turn to see that he was also unlacing his leather pants.

"I don't know shit about you or what you might or might not do. I'm not just going to take your word for it," I snap and swim back further into the pool. I tell myself that if things start to go bad, I will at least buy myself some time to escape if they have to get their pants off before they can hurt me. Besides, the last thing I need right now is to deal with their dicks and any effect *they* might have on my already conflicting desires.

Zeph and Ryn stare at each other for a second, and then Ryn shrugs and Zeph rolls his eyes. He grumbles something that I can't make out and steps into the pool with his pants on. I get that Zeph thinks I'm some kind of spy for who the fuck only knows, but I have to wonder if he's this much of a prick all the time or if this surly shit is just for me. Ryn follows him into the water, and I take a deep measured breath to prepare myself for round two of *let's fuck with Falon's hormones*.

"Drink this," Ryn orders me as he walks toward me and extends his hand. He's holding a small clear glass vial with light pink liquid in it.

I stare at him, making no effort to take it. "Right, I'm just going to down that with no questions, being that I'm all for giving you fuckers the benefit of the doubt," I tell him, my nose scrunching up with distaste.

Ryn rolls his eyes at me now. "This just encourages the truth," he tells me and then presses the vial closer. I lean away from it automatically, and Ryn lets out an irritated huff. He brings the vial to his lips and takes a sip. "See, it's not poison or anything that's going to hurt you," he reassures once again, and I watch him warily for any signs that he's lying.

I reach out and take the vial and bring it up to my nose and sniff. It smells like yellow cake, and I drop it to my lips and tilt my head back to drink the whole thing like a shot. A cool sensation spreads out inside of me, and I lick my lips as I hand the vial back to Ryn.

"What did it taste like to you?" he asks me oddly.

"Like yellow cake," I answer, and I don't miss the look that Ryn gives to Zeph who moves to my right. "Motherfuckers!" I shout at them and splash them both with water as I turn and try to swim away. Of course, their giant selves can fucking walk in this pool, and they stride toward me faster than I can swim away. "If you fucking roofied me, I'm going to kill you both. I don't care if you're the size of a mountain. I will find a bulldozer or a stick of dynamite or something. Not even mountains withstand that shit!"

I fight against the big hands that wrap around my waist and pull me backwards. I kick and flail, splashing around like a hooked shark desperate for escape. "I will go full House of Tyrell Sand Snake on your mountain asses, and you'll be the ones getting your heads crushed. I will fucking crush your heads!" I screech as my back slams into the warm wet chest of either Zeph or Ryn. My threats become unintelligible as I battle to get out of my captor's grip and curse them to hell and back.

I'm not sure how long I struggle or how long they just stand there and let me. I realize that it's Zeph who's holding me tightly to him like he's trying to swaddle me with his body in order to get me to calm down, and I hate that it's working. Tears prick my eyes again as I uselessly try to get away and he exerts very little effort to keep me right where I am. I stop screaming at them and breathe hard, trying to keep the feeling of helplessness and vulnerability from drowning me.

"You useless fucking pigeon," I shout at my gryphon, turning my rage on her. "I *wish* you were a wolf instead of a rotisserie chicken, you worthless buffalo wing!" I jibe, hoping for some kind of response. *Any* kind of response, but nothing stirs inside of me.

Ryn's eyes widen with surprise as I turn my impotent

rage on my animal instead of them, cursing her and threatening her. I even fucking try bribery, but nothing. I feel fucking nothing inside where she should clearly be.

As a teenager, I had to come to terms with being latent when I realized I couldn't shift, but I always felt what I thought was a wolf inside of me. The connection with my animal was there even if I couldn't unlock her. I had the heightened smell and hearing, the strength and dominance. I always felt her. But now I've shifted into some winged fucking monster, and suddenly I'm empty inside. If this whole being held captive thing isn't enough to scare the shit out of me, the loneliness I now feel in my chest trumps that fear a million fold.

Where are you?

I plead with my gryphon, but it's met with stillness and silence inside of me, my desperation clearly not enough to make anything happen. The bitch has abandoned me, and I hate her for it.

7

I give up and go still in Zeph's hold. I pant through my desolation and meet Ryn's gaze with defeat in my eyes. He almost looks sorry.

"If you're done now, I'll just scrub you, and then we'll ask some questions," he tells me, his tone a little softer, and I don't bother to wipe at the tear that streaks down my cheek. Another follows in its tracks, unchecked, and I look away from him and stare out into the darkening forest.

I don't say or do anything as Ryn scrubs my face, neck and shoulders with soft moss that smells like hopelessness. I don't fight Zeph as he loosens his hold and lifts my arms or when he spins me around so that Ryn can scrub my back when he's done with the front of me. I don't look at Zeph. Don't give him a peek of the desolation coursing through my every cell, but I can feel his honey gaze on me the whole time. They say nothing as they scrub me down quickly and efficiently, and the silence constricts around us even tighter as no one says or does anything for a minute after it's clear Ryn is done.

Zeph slowly spins me around, my back against his chest again. "What is your name?" he asks me eventually, his deep tone snaking its way unwelcomingly through me and leaving warmth in its wake.

"Falon Solei Umbra," I answer robotically.

"And where are you from?" Ryn presses.

"Colorado. That's a state in the USA which is located on the North American continent," I repeat.

"Are you Avowed?" Zeph grumbles out.

I blink away another tear. "I don't think so, but I don't exactly know what that is, so I can't say for sure."

"Are you mated?" Zeph asks me, and something about his tone or the question makes me snap out of my cyborg impression.

"No," I growl out, meeting Ryn's eyes in front of me with pure rage.

"What were you doing flying through the Amaranthine Mountains?" Zeph demands.

"I don't know," I admit. "I was trying to spread my grand-mother's ashes, but all of a sudden, I felt like I'd been hit by lightning. The next thing I know, I had wings, and you were attacking me," I accuse and look up over my shoulder at him. I'm pressed too closely against him, and all I can make out is his five-o'clock-shadow-dusted chin.

"What do you know of Lazza?" Ryn asks me, and I pull my irritated glare from Zeph's chin and rest it back on Ryn's gray eyes.

"I don't know who that is. I've only heard the name once before when *he* mentioned it," I say, gesturing with my head to indicate Zeph behind me.

"What about Vedan or Kestrel City? The Ouphe?" Ryn presses.

I shrug. "No idea what any of that means."

Ryn and Zeph exchange a confused look and an incred-ulous laugh escapes me. "You were so convinced that I was lying, but I wasn't. I told you assholes the truth the first time you asked me for it! Stupid pricks," I sling at them and push out of Zeph's hold. "Get the fuck off me," I snap at him, and I'm surprised when he actually lets me go. I swim away from them toward the edge of the pool and then turn around, leaving the rocky edge to protect my back.

"Can I fucking go home now?" I demand, completely fed up with everything that's happened from the minute I woke up in this strange place.

"No," Ryn answers, and my stare snaps to his in surprise. He looks about as shocked as I do.

"Why not?" I question.

"Because you belong to us now," he tells me, and then he slaps a hand over his mouth.

"Wait. What?"

"What he means is we don't know how to get you home. There are old stories of gates that the Ouphe used to pass to different places, but the knowledge of how to use them died when they did. We don't know how you got here," Zeph tells me, stepping in front of Ryn.

"Is that true?" I ask, looking past Zeph and focusing on Ryn.

"Yes," he tells me, and an emphatic nod punctuates the word.

"Can you figure it out?" I press. "I have a job and a life." I open my mouth to try and say that I want to go home, but nothing comes out. I furrow my brow in confusion and look to Zeph and Ryn for help.

"You can't say things that are untrue," Zeph tells me, and he runs his gaze over my face.

But I want to go home, I tell myself and then try to communicate that once more. Nothing comes out. *What the fuck?* "You're a dick," I blurt to Zeph, checking to make sure that my ability to speak hasn't somehow been taken from me.

His dour features turn downright cantankerous, and he runs a wet hand through his black curls. "So what exactly are we supposed to do with her now?" he snarls and turns to Ryn. Ryn's eyes widen in panic. "Don't answer that," Zeph commands quickly, and I stare back and forth between them for a minute.

"She's not one of Lazza's. She's not Avowed. She should stay here where she'll be safe until we can sort things out," Ryn finally offers, and I can tell that's the last thing that Zeph wants to hear.

I look around trying to think through any other alternative to being here with these mountain-sized assholes, but until I can figure out exactly what *here* means in relation to where I come from, my hands are tied. That thought sends a spark of heat flashing through me, and I roll my eyes at this new side of me that could put a nympho to shame. Zeph and Ryn are whisper arguing about something that I can't make out, and I ignore it as I pull myself out of the water and reach for the fawn-colored shirt that Ryn had on under his armored vest.

I pull it on, glad to find that it falls past my ass to mid-thigh, and fight the sudden drive I feel to bring the fabric up to my nose and inhale it. "Fuck, I need to get laid," I observe, and I pull my now white hair over one shoulder and wring it out into the water.

The whisper arguing suddenly stops, and I look down into the water to find both Ryn and Zeph staring at me. I can't quite decipher the look they're both wearing, but it's not flattering, given what I just said.

"Don't worry, that wasn't an invitation." I open my mouth to tell them I wouldn't even touch their dicks with somebody else's vagina, but I can't get the words out. "How long before this shit wears off?" I ask and point to my mouth.

suddenly pulled into my back, and I have to slam a hand over my mouth to stifle my yip of happiness.

Fuck yeah, take that, wings! I own you now!

I cheer in my mind and then cross my fingers and fucking hope that's now true. I sit up and lean back against a pillar that separates the balcony from the room inside and release a deep weary exhale. I rest my head back and close my eyes, and my grandmother's face appears on the back of my eyelids. She never smiled much, and a stern unyielding face stares back at me. Her white hair is pulled away from her face tightly, and I know if she turns around, I'll find a braid that falls almost to the small of her back.

Her aqua gaze reads me like a book, just as it always did, and the lines around her eyes deepen as she stares at me.

"Why not tell me, Gran?" I ask my memory of her. "Why all this cloak and dagger shit?" The image says nothing, which doesn't surprise me, as figments of my imagination can't supply answers that I don't have. I stare at my grandmother a little longer as if the answers lie somewhere in the grooves that time etched into her face, but I'm still as in the dark as I was when I first woke up in this strange place. Well, maybe not *that* in the dark, I do know that I'm a gryphon, and Zeph and Ryn now know I'm not a spy, so there's that at least. I hear Zeph bellow a faint command, and I resist the urge to peek and see if they're outside scrambling or somewhere in the cliff castle freaking out.

I can picture the two of them, all grumpy and irritated at being thwarted, and I bite down against the chuckle that spills out of my mouth. The image of them barking commands and searching for me is the last thing that floats through my mind before my weary body and mind succumb to sleep.

8

Sirens yank me from my deep and bliss-filled slumber. I sit up, panic slamming into me, and a yellow sheet slips off my torso and pools at my waist. I look around at the familiar room.

How the fuck did I get back here?

I'm naked again, and I roll my eyes and release a growl. Why the hell do I keep waking up like this? I pull the top sheet off and wrap it around me. I stumble out onto the balcony, trying to figure out what the hell is going on, and have to duck to avoid getting decapitated by a massive wing as a gryphon whooshes past me. Another one flies by, and I notice that it's decked out in armor. I look over the railing of the balcony to find other gryphons being fitted in the clearing at the base of the cliff.

The alarm is quieter out here on the balcony, but I see people scrambling into the cliff castle and others scrambling out, shifting, and waiting for someone to fit them with armor. I look up at the sky, figuring whatever is setting off these alarms must be coming from somewhere up there, but I don't see anything other than blue skies and an occasional wispy cloud. Another gryphon that's been fitted and kitted flies past me to disappear up and over the waterfall.

My gryphon starts to stir, and I focus on that for a minute, trying to discern what it is that captured her attention enough to make her show up. I'm not sure if it's the alarm of the other gryphons setting her off, but part of me wants to try to coax her the rest of the way to the surface and follow the other gryphons to see what's going on. Another part of me knows that would be a really stupid idea, especially since my animal is a dick and seems to take great joy in fucking me over.

The door to the room slams open behind me, and I move to shield myself with a pillar. A throat clears.

"I can see the trail of your blanket, milady," a feminine voice informs me, and I peek to the side of the pillar to find Tysa standing there holding a pile of peach fabric. Her brown eyes are filled with amusement, and her cute pouty lips are turned up in a half smile.

I wave awkwardly at her and then step out from behind my bad choice of hiding spots. "Hey, sorry, I thought you were maybe Zeph or Ryn," I explain as I approach her. "Apparently, I suck at hide and seek," I add, gesturing to the bed I have no idea how I ended up in.

"We should get you dressed, milady, and then join the others until the all clear is given," Tysa urges me, fanning out the fabric in her hands, which appears to be some kind of dress.

The alarm still ringing through the room has me nodding and unwrapping the sheet from around myself. I would try to get dressed myself, but whatever is in Tysa's hands looks complicated, and I'm just happy to have clothes again. She holds the dress down for me, and I quickly step into it. I have no idea what it's made of, but it's the softest material I've ever felt. The gathered peach fabric has been sewn onto a rose gold chain, and Tysa fastens it around my neck.

"Loa said to make you something straight from the walking paths of Kestrel. I stayed up all night and made two gowns that should work, but I can take some measurements from you today and start on some more tonight," Tysa tells me, and I can hear the nervous tension in her rambling. She attaches something to the back of the chain around my neck, and then I feel her wrap another cool metal chain around my lower back, bringing it forward to cinch the peach fabric just below my belly button.

"There," she tells me, stepping back and admiring her hard work, excitement sparkling in her eyes.

I'm not sure what to say, but the fact of the matter is, I was more covered by the sheet than I am by this *dress*. The fabric fastened at my neck is pulled tightly around my breasts and cinched below my belly button. There is nothing covering the side of my ribs, and the fabric drapes down well past my hips on both sides. The chain belt at my waist is the only thing keeping the gathered fabric from billowing out and flashing my vagina. The tops of my ass cheeks are visible from the low side drapes, but my crack is hidden by the part of the dress that runs up my spine and connects to the back of the chain at my neck.

I'm two chain breaks away from being naked.

"Very fitting of the highborn that you are, milady," Tysa tells me, and as uncomfortable as I am, there's no way in hell that I'm dousing the pride I see in her gaze.

"Call me Falon," I encourage. "And I'm about as far as you can get from highborn," I add, uncomfortable with all this *milady* shit.

Tysa looks at me confused. "But your hair?"

I run my fingers through the tangled tresses and pull it forward. It's still a little shocking to see that it's white with hints of light gray in it now. "Do all the highborn have white hair?"

"The women do, milady. Some buy wigs or pay a year's worth of my wages to have a treatment done every month, but the purest mixes of Ouphe blood give the girls white hair. They're bred specifically for that trait in the females."

I'm confused by what she's saying, but she hands me a brush and then hurries me out of the room, the alarm punctuating our urgent steps. I speed walk to keep up with Tysa's longer stride and try to make sure my private bits stay tucked in and hidden. I'm led to the same massive room I was brought to yesterday for questioning, and I tense a little as I picture the table full of douchebags and their questions. Tysa leads me through the carved wooden doors, and I find that the room is now filled with people who are whispering frantically and wearing worry on their faces.

"I'll grab you some food from the kitchens," Tysa informs me and then disappears back out the door before I can say anything or beg her not to leave me alone.

I've never been one who was super comfortable in large social gatherings, and when you add in that I still have no idea where I am and know no one, I'm feeling a little awkward, to say the least. I make my way through the crowd, giving a small friendly smile to a guy I make eye contact with. He glares at me and then quickly turns away. Conversations become hushed as I get closer, and after a couple more glares and angry dismissals, I feel even more tense and awkward.

"Ahh, I was wondering if you'd be joining us or them," Loa announces as she spots me and makes her way in my direction.

I don't know who the *them* are that she's referring to, but based on the sneer she's wearing, I don't think she's talking about the armored gryphons. Loa stops in front of me, her frame towering, and she runs her gaze up and down my body.

"I'm glad to see Tysa was able to accommodate your...tastes," Loa taunts, and it's clear by the way she says *tastes*, she's insinuating I don't have any. I look around and see that I'm very overdressed—or maybe I should say under-dressed—among this crowd, and I raise a knowing eyebrow at Loa.

This bitch.

"Yeah, Tysa's a rare talent," I tell her casually, not showing any of the discomfort or irritation I'm currently feeling. "It was so very kind of you to order this dress for me. I'll be sure to think of plenty of ways I can repay your generosity," I reply, my tone sweet, my gaze threatening. It doesn't take a genius to know that the term *highborn* is a dirty word amongst these people and that Loa just hardcore fucked with my chances of fitting in here.

Or maybe my new white hair did that. Either way, I really want to get the fuck out of here, and as soon as I do, I'm ripping this dress off. I don't care if I have to wear a sheet until I can get home; I don't like how these people are looking at me, and the last thing I need is to be more of a target here.

The alarm goes quiet, and it's enough of a distraction for me to slip past the tree-sized bitch, Loa, and make my way to a spot by the window. Relief washes through the crowd in the room, and the somber conversations quickly morph into more animated ones. Tysa finds me leaning against the wall and hands me a plate of food, none of which I can identify. I start with what I hope is a roll, figuring it's probably the safest bet.

"Holy shit, that's good!" I mumble with a full mouth as the soft buttery inside melts in my mouth with just a hint of sweetness. I proceed to stuff my face, not even caring that

I'm eating like some starved animal, because I am, in fact, a starved animal.

"So, Tysa, can you fill me in on what the hell is going on here? I mean, going off of what I've been accused of and the sirens and shit, it seems like there's some kind of battle going on, but I'm clearly missing a lot here," I confess, and Tysa pulls on my hand, indicating that she wants me to sit down next to her.

I do, setting my plateful of food in my barely covered lap and attempt to slow down the ravenous stuffing of my face so I don't choke. I bring a piece of what looks like some kind of turquoise fruit up to my nose and sniff it a couple times. I figure since it doesn't smell like shit, it probably doesn't taste like shit, so I put that theory to the test and take a small hesitant bite. I pump my fist when I discover that it tastes like the sweetest pineapple mixed with the sweetest strawberry I've ever tasted. I close my eyes and savor the new flavor.

"We are the Hidden," she tells me and gestures to the room full of people. "We are gryphons who refuse to take the vow or bend the knee to unworthy leaders."

I wait for her to elaborate, but she seems content with that explanation. "What makes them unworthy," I ask, and a male close to us turns around and glares hard at me. "I'm not saying they aren't; I'm just trying to understand," I defend against the murderous look the stranger is now sending my way.

"It's a really long story, but the Ouphe used to control and use us. We were required to enter into a vow of servitude at just sixteen. We fought for a very long time to break from that enslavement and from those practices, but our people are divided about the vow itself. Some leaders think that we should still swear fealty and take the mark of our ancestors. They pretend it's to honor the original vow and the magic a gryphon can access if they make it. But really it's so that the highbloods that have enough Ouphe blood in their veins can still control the rest of us."

Tysa spits on the ground like she's trying to rid herself of the taste of those words.

"We are the rebels that are fighting against that. We fight against control in all forms and the loss of our will. We are the Hidden," she tells me once again, and this time, I look at the people in this room with a new understanding.

"And the alarms?" I query.

"They could mean a lot of things. A prisoner escape." She stares at me pointedly, and I chuckle around a mouthful of some kind of meat that's spicy and delicious. "It could be that we're under attack, although the old magic in this mountain makes that unlikely. It could mean a returning patrol needs help, or the Avowed requesting a meet. We don't fall for that trick much anymore though."

I look around at the light smooth stone of the room and wonder what she means by *old magic in this mountain.* I notice something that looks like writing in the inside arch of the window, and one of the symbols triggers something in me. I stare at it, suddenly struck by the feeling that happens when a word sits on the tip of my tongue, but I just can't seem to wrap my mouth around it. It looks so fucking familiar, and yet I can't seem to place it.

A loud boom pulses through the room, and a couple people give surprised screams, including me. It's a good thing I've quickly cleaned off almost everything except for some gray sludge on my plate, or it would have just gone flying all over me. Everyone looks around, but no one seems to know what the hell just happened. Gryphons suddenly appear at the windows, talons and claws gripping the sills as their bird-like heads search the room. Tysa and I scurry to our feet at their sudden appearance, and I'm taken aback by their size. The cutouts in the wall are massive and span the entire length, and yet these gryphons are still too big to fit through them.

I stare at them in awe, their features similar, but each of their colorings so different and unique from one another. *Is my gryphon this mammoth as well?* I wonder as I watch one of the new window visitors flap his wings to help him keep his balance. I want to step forward and touch one, but I also don't want to lose a hand.

Behind me, the closed doors leading into the room fly open, slamming against the stone wall, and everyone jumps and screams again. It's like we're all watching a thriller movie, and every little thing that jumps out scares the shit out of the whole theater. I stifle a chuckle at the thought.

A shirtless Zeph storms into the massive room. Loa and some other familiar faces I recognize from the interrogation yesterday all shoot to attention and move to surround him. My gaze travels of its own accord from Zeph's mussed up black curls to his strong shoulders. Muscles cord thickly around his arms and then they dip and tease my eyes at his bare chest and stomach. I lick my lips and tilt my head appreciatively. A small growl sneaks out of my mouth when someone steps in front of me and blocks my view.

The sound I'm suddenly emitting startles me, and the shock snaps me out of the eye fuck that was just happening. A low chuckle from the big bare chest in front of me has my eyes snapping up to meet an amused gray gaze.

"Altern," Tysa greets Ryn with a curtsey.

I roll my eyes at the display which is probably dumb of me. I should be trying to learn about their customs and fit in here. Maybe if they like me, they'll be more helpful in my quest to find my way back home. But the thought of curt-seying to Ryn or Zeph gets my feathers all ruffled with irritation, and I can't actually picture myself doing it.

Ryn gives Tysa a nod and a smile that has her blushing. I feel the sudden need to slap him, and I clench my fist to stop myself. It's like *Invasion of the Body Snatchers* up in here, only it's just *me* fighting against this new seriously horny and possessive stranger inside of me. It's fucking annoying. I growl at Tysa because something inside of me decided she blinked too much in Ryn's direction, and then slam a hand over my mouth because *what the fuck!* My eyes widen and fill with apology, and Tysa's brown gaze snaps to mine.

"I'm mated, milady. I would never..." she stammers, and I feel even worse.

"I never thought you would," I quickly reassure her and then realize what I just said. "I mean, you can if you want, I don't fucking care. That's between you and your mate. I don't even know what that was," I say gesturing to my mouth. "I think I had some serious indigestion or something, and that was just a gnarly burp," I ramble until Ryn's chuckle has us both turning to look at him.

He's staring at me, his storm cloud gray eyes twinkling with amusement. Maybe I'm so used to being looked at with suspicion and disdain by him—and pretty much everyone else here except maybe Tysa—but I'm stunned silent by how beautiful he looks when he's smiling. I almost fucking gasp with how taken I am by it, and that just pisses me off. Why am I all swoony these days? I like to fuck. I like pleasure and flirting and the chase. I do not fucking swoon. That weak-in-the-knees shit is for romcoms and needy bitches. I am as far as you can get from needy.

Ryn's eyes run down my body, and his gaze looks momentarily bewildered before he starts to blush. The pink moves up his chest, past his neck, and creeps slowly into his cheeks. When he looks back up, his eyes are banked with want, and his hands twitch at his sides.

I glare at him.

"Like it?" I challenge, lifting my arms and doing a little spin so he can see all angles, and I can catch my breath for a moment from that heated look in his eyes. "Loa had Tysa make it for me. What was it you said, Tysa, oh that's right, something worthy of a highborn straight from the streets of Kestrel. Wherever the hell that is," I grumble as I spin.

I almost choke on the words when Ryn reaches out and runs his index finger over the bare skin of my lower hip. My clit gives my vagina a green light to start her engines at his touch, but I slap his hand away because I know I can't trust those instincts.

Ryn looks at me, shocked, and I can't tell if he just realized that he was touching me or he's shocked that I just batted his hand away. Either way, I'm trying very hard not to care. My nipples pebble, and I know it will be obvious through the top of this dress. I force myself to think of shit that isn't sexy and isn't fuel for the flames, but I keep flashing back to the pools and me in the center of a Ryn and Zeph sandwich.

"I've never been overly fond of the fashion of Kestrel, but I can appreciate that what it lacks in practicality, it makes up for with..." he trails off for a second in thought. "Appeal. This is an image worth saving," he tells Tysa and taps at his temple.

Her smile turns beaming, and I'm both happy for her and trying to figure out if Ryn just said what I thought he did. I shoo my thoughts away from exactly what Ryn might be doing with the images he's saving in his mind of me in this dress, and turn to Tysa.

"Instead of more beautiful dresses, do you think you could make me some pants and a couple shirts?" I ask. "I don't have any money, but I'm a mechanic, and if you have anything that needs fixing, I would gladly trade my services for yours."

Tysa mouths the word *mechanic* right after I say it. She looks puzzled, but it seems, the word *fixing* she understands, and her brown eyes light up with excitement. "Really?" she queries, and her unbridled enthusiasm makes me suddenly uncertain of what I'm promising.

"Yeah, I mean, I'm pretty handy, but even I have my limits. If it's within my power and ability, I'd be happy to trade my help for some pants and shirts," I agree, trying to be clearer on the terms of what I'm offering and expecting in return.

"Yes!" Tysa exclaims. "By all the stars in the sky, yes, I accept." She curtsies and then starts to bounce away. She immediately comes back and curtsies in front of Ryn. "Are we all clear, Altern?" she asks, and when he nods yes, she scurries away again.

I watch her hurriedly weave through the people and out the door. I look back at Ryn who's now wearing a cheeky smile and, once again, feel unsure of exactly what I've agreed to. I shrug, I guess I'll find out soon enough. If it's something I can't do, then no pants for me. I'll just have to deal with these two dresses. I look down at the strips of fabric barely covering me and cringe. I don't know what the other dress Tysa made even looks like. I just hope it's not more revealing than this one.

Please let whatever Tysa wants to be fixed be like a toaster or something, I plea silently.

A breeze sneaks in through the window we're standing next to, and white strands of my hair tickle my cheek and neck. Ryn reaches out and catches one between his thumb and index finger and rubs it gently. It reminds me of when he was running his hands through my hair yesterday, and goose bumps rise up on my arms. I slap his hand away again, and evidently, he finds that amusing. He takes a step toward me, and my breathing picks up. I feel panicked and excited simultaneously, and I don't know what that fucking means.

"Come, Falon Solei Umbra," he practically purrs, and the way his lips and tongue caress my name feels naughty and inviting. "I'll show you around," Ryn tells me, and he turns on his heel and starts to saunter through the thinning crowd.

I watch him for a beat as he weaves his way toward the doors. He doesn't even look back, he's so certain I'll follow him. I feel eyes on me, and I scan the room to find Loa and Zeph's stares both fixed on me. Zeph's eyes start to dip down my body, but they snap back up suddenly like he just realized what he was doing and put a stop to it. He glares at me like I've wronged him in some way, and I bristle against the vitriol seeping out of his golden honey gaze. I flip him and Loa the bird and then follow in Ryn's wake, eager to get the hell out of this room and start figuring things out.

9

"So what was all that about?" I ask, gesturing behind me with one of the rolls I just jacked from the kitchen tour.

With all the stairs in this place Ryn has me trekking up and down, I need all the calories I can get at this point. Ryn gives me the side-eye as I swallow down another chipmunk-cheek inducing bite. I ignore his judgement; I'm starving. It's like the plate of food Tysa already fed me was just an appetizer and now I'm ready for the main course. As soon as Ryn finishes showing me the courtyard or wherever he's taking me right now, I'm headed back to the kitchen and camping out there until this gnawing need in my stomach is sated.

"What was *what* all about?" Ryn queries as we hike up several flights of stairs until I'm winded, and the sound of the waterfall that pours off the cliff castle pounds through every surface around us. I can barely hear past my deep gasps for air, let alone him, so I wait until we start making our way through some cave and things are a little quieter to elaborate.

"The alarms, armored gryphons, and the mysterious

explosion? What was that all about?" I clarify as I scan the rocky ground in the dim light for anything I might trip over.

"We were just running a drill. That happens from time to time here. We can never be too prepared for anything and everything the Avowed may throw at us," he tells me matter-of-factly.

"Yeah, Tysa was telling me about them and the Oh-f," I try to say, but the word is a jumble of wrong in my mouth.

"The Ouphe," Ryn corrects me, and I say it over and over again until it feels natural against my tongue and lips. I smile when I get it right and look over at Ryn like I'm expecting a cookie or a gold star or something. His eyes jump up to mine from where he was just staring fixated at my lips, and then he quickly looks away, refocusing on his path through the cave. I'm getting the distinct impression that Ryn is DTF, but that doesn't make a lot of sense to me as he was all about the hate yesterday.

"Uh...anyway," I continue. "Tysa made it seem like all the evil, enslaving Ouphe were all dead. What happened to them?" I press and proceed to finish the last of my roll stash.

"The warring tribes of Ouphe killed each other off, for the most part. Some groups escaped through the gates, and we hunted the rest that stayed behind." Ryn states all of this very casually as we make our way closer to the light-filled exit. The brutality of the word *hunt* stands out to me and gives me the chills. I'm not sure why it makes me feel uncomfortable; I don't know the Ouphe or the Gryphons really. Who am I to judge their history and how it was handled?

"It's rumored that some small tribes found shelter up in the Quietus Mountains, but they know better than to cross paths with us. And really, it's all probably just a rumor; those lands are practically uninhabitable."

I nod in agreement and then chuckle at myself. I have no

fucking clue if it's true or not, so I have no idea why I'm just agreeing with him.

"Now, I heard the sirens, but what explosion were you talking abou—" Ryn starts, but my gasp cuts him off as we exit the cave and step out into the sun.

I look around me, wide-eyed, taking it all in. It's so green and beautiful I don't even know what to stare at first. The short grass looks soft enough to sleep on. It's some kind of mix between pillowy looking moss and the bladed green stuff that exists back home. The wind blows a cool mist over me from the river that leaps off the edge of the cliff and thunders down the side of the cliff castle. I close my eyes and revel in the feel of it as faint shouts reach my ears. I open my eyes and take in the deep periwinkle of the water that stretches as far as I can see.

"Is this an island?" I ask, curious and not able to contain it.

"No, we just kiss the Talle Lake in quite a few places," Ryn offers, and he makes his way toward some trees to the right.

This is a lake? I question as I stare past the top of the cliff we're on and take in the expanse of water. *It's the biggest lake I've ever seen.* I move to follow Ryn and have to bite back a moan as I step out onto the soft grass. It feels like a layer of cotton against the sore pads of my feet, and I have the sudden urge to roll around in it. The wind picks up, making my hair and the fabric of my barely there dress dance about, and I almost flash nipple when the sneaky air tries to get randy with the gathered part of the dress covering my boobs.

Note to self: roll around in the soft grass when Tysa gives me pants and tops. Until then, try to keep the girls covered and the sideboob in check.

"So you thought you were a wolf?" Ryn asks over his

shoulder, but I'm distracted by my nipples' attempts to escape.

"What?" I ask as I position things back where they're supposed to be. I slam into something hard and bounce back unbalanced. Ryn grabs my hips to keep me from introducing my ass to the soft grass.

"What are you doing?" he queries as I expel the last of the *oomph* that escapes me from crashing into his back. There's a twinkle of something in his storm-gray eyes, and I'm suddenly aware of just how pressed up against him I am. I can feel the texture of the scaled and braided leather he's wearing against my stomach and hardening nipples.

"Playing with my boobs," I blurt, and Ryn barks out a laugh and tightens his grip on my hips. My very bare hips, I observe, as the rough skin of his palms lights up a plethora of sensations in me. His laughter snakes through me, keying me up like it's my favorite song. My clit pulses with anticipation as I clench around emptiness. I start to breathe through the shit ton of need that just tsunami'd through me. I want to fuck him. I want him to snap the two chains holding this poor excuse for a dress together and then slam me up against the tree and make me scream. I want a back full of bark, blood, and scratches from how hard he fucks me.

The need to know if he tastes like the rain clouds that are in his eyes drives me to rise up on my tip toes, and I lick my bottom lip in invitation. Ryn leans down, as transfixed by the moment and—judging by his dilated pupils—as driven with need as I currently am. His full lips are just a hair's breadth away, and I can feel the promise of pleasure and the need to own and dominate in his grip and on his breath as it caresses my mouth. A pained shout reverberates through the trees around us, and Ryn suddenly blinks and then pulls away from me. Like a desperate dumbass, I lean forward chasing his retreating lips for a second before coming to my senses and realizing what I'm doing.

His hands release my hips, and the tips of his fingers skate over my now heated skin as he pulls away. I try to clear my head of the lust clouding my every thought right now. *What the fuck am I doing?* My red alert alarm sounds off in my head about three minutes too late. I push away from him, disconnecting any part of me that's still touching any part of him, and if I didn't know any better, I'd say he almost reaches out for me before he fists his hand and drops it back by his side.

Another shout slithers through the trees to find us, and I expect Ryn to hurry off in its direction, but he doesn't. He just stands there.

"You thought you were a wolf?" he asks me, and the question feels so out of left field that it takes me a moment to catch it and examine what he's asking.

"Yeah, that's what my gran always told me. I always smelled like one before..." I trail off as once again the image of the disintegrating ring pops into my head.

"What was her name?" Ryn asks, pulling me from my thoughts.

"My gran's?"

He nods.

"Sedora Steward," I offer and watch his face for any hint of recognition. My gran was clearly keeping things from me, and I can't help but think maybe she was from here and her name might be recognized.

Nothing akin to knowing lights up in Ryn's gray eyes. He just furrows his brow in thought and then turns and continues to make his way through the trees. Ten feet later, I step into a clearing the size of two football fields. On the end closest to us, boys and girls who all look to be teenagers hack away at each other with wooden swords. Grunts and shouts fill the air as the clack of wood and the thump of hits swirl around me. Beyond this sword fighting group is another group where people are wrestling each other. All the way on the other side are shifted gryphons who also seem to be taking turns having a go at each other.

"Well, Falon Solei Umbra, you're not a wolf, you're a gryphon, and it's time you learn just what that means."

This time, when Ryn says my name, there's no sexy caress to it. No, this time it feels saturated with mockery and topped off with challenge. Ryn walks away from me like he's thrown down the gauntlet and has nothing else to say, but his challenge isn't one of those *you got this and I believe in you* kinds. It's more of a *meh, if you die, that's one less problem I have to deal with.* I watch him walk away, and the simple arrogance in his stride has me wanting to pick up the nearby rock I spot and chuck it at his head. I stop myself, just barely. Knowing my luck though, I'd miss him completely, and the rock would bounce off a tree and take *me* out instead, or worse, hurt one of the kids practicing here. That's just what I need—some momma gryphon coming for me.

I stand there not sure what else to do. He didn't say follow, and he didn't say stay. The fact that I feel like a misplaced puppy right now is really fucking annoying. I watch the kids, at least I think they're kids, sparring back and forth with their wooden swords, some of them elegant and smooth like a proper fencer would be, and some of them hacking away at their opponent, their brute strength just as much of a weapon as the sword in their hand is. It's hard to tell if my initial teenager instinct is correct. They look young in the face, but they're all about my size, some of them even bigger. It's clear that gryphons are a larger people than humans are.

I've been so used to being a *very tall woman* amidst humans and shifters back home. However, here, I'm practically a runt. A yelp sounds off to my right, and immediately my eyes snap in its direction. A kid flicks his wrist just so, and his opponent's weapon flies up in the air and arcs toward him where he snatches it from the air easily. I recognize the skilled swordsman as the walking, talking lie detector test that Zeph summoned at my interrogation. Ami, I think, was his name, or maybe it was Amit or Amish or something *A*. Shit, why do I suck at names so badly?

Whatever-his-name-is hands the sword he just stole from his opponent back and readies himself for another round of Medieval Fighting 101. I strain to watch them reengage, but I spot Ryn walking back toward me with another bigfoot of a gryphon shifter, and suddenly they're all I can focus on. Ryn's cocky swagger is in place and on display, but it's the guy he's talking to that I focus on. *What the hell do they feed these guys? Steroids?*

He has long, gold-streaked, chestnut-colored hair that's pulled back at his nape. He has a beard that's just past short and just shy of unkempt, and his sage-tinted gaze is focused as he listens to whatever it is that Ryn's telling him, while also keeping his focus on the sword wielding trainees. His gait is powerful and assured, lacking the cocky bounce of the asshole gryphon next to him. They come to a stop in front of me.

"This is her," Ryn announces, like I'm unworthy now of having my name in his mouth. I glare at him as the big guy finally takes his attention from the sparring kids and brings it to me. His eyes immediately widen with shock, and he snaps his head in Ryn's direction.

"This is an eyas?" he asks, confused, turning back to me like he's double-checking if he's right. He runs his sage green eyes down my frame, and I can see the moment my lack of clothing registers. His Adam's apple bobs as he swallows, and he shifts his weight like he's uncomfortable, folding and then unfolding his arms.

"Trust me, she is," Ryn assures him. "The little thing can barely fly," he adds, looking at me with mock sympathy.

"If you'd stop trying to cuddle with me midair, maybe I could," I volley back sweetly, even though in my head I'm pummeling the asshole. "What the fuck is an eyas?" I demand, not sure if they're insulting me.

"It's what we call our young," the hot trainer answers and then returns his confused gaze to Ryn. "She's high-born," he suddenly objects, and I turn my glare on him.

Ryn shrugs. "She has the features, but no mark. She's not even from here. Zeph found her near a gate. So until we can get rid of her, she's your problem," Ryn declares, and the trainer and I both round on him in shock. "Eyas, this is Sutton. Sutton this is the eyas. Get to work," he orders and starts to walk away.

Sutton opens his mouth to say something, but I don't hear what when a stinging slap lands on my ass cheek. *Did this motherfucker just slap my ass?* My hands fly to cover my stinging glute, and I spin and leap at Ryn's back. My gryphon of course does jack diddly shit, but I don't give a fuck if she sits this one out; I'm going to rip him apart if it's the last thing I do. A feral growl bursts out of me as I soar closer to my target, but all of a sudden, I'm plucked out of the air like a pouncing cat and pulled back into a hard body.

I fight and snap to get out of Sutton's hold, and then I seriously lose my shit when Ryn fucking looks at me over his shoulder and smiles.

"Cut that out, Ryn, or I'll let her go," Sutton warns, and I'm mildly pleased to see Ryn's smile waver slightly before he turns around and disappears through the trees. I scramble and continue to try and go after Ryn while Sutton does his best to calm me. "Hey there, little bit, I can't have you attacking the Altern on my watch, so you just have to let it go. I can teach you how to best him, but this isn't the way to do it," he coaxes, and the last statement gets my attention.

Like he can feel some of the fight in me waning, his voice gets even more encouraging and kind. "Stick with me, little bit, I'll get you more vicious than a Thais Fairy in no time. Give you more bite to back up that growl, whatta ya think, huh?"

I sag against him, defeat coursing through me. I'm so fucking tired of feeling like this. "Can you teach me to never be helpless again?" I ask, and the pain in my question rises to the surface, coating the anger I poured into my words. I feel Sutton release a deep breath against me, and I can practically feel the empathy radiating off him.

"There will always be someone bigger and meaner, but if you work hard, I can teach you to shred anyone who gets in your way."

I nod at that, and Sutton's hold on me loosens. He sets me on my feet, and then we both realize that in my efforts to get away and his efforts to stop me, Sutton is firmly holding on to one of my boobs. He yanks his hand away as if I just burned him, and I turn around to find him slowly reddening like a ripening tomato.

"My apologies," he stammers out, and the whole situation suddenly seems really funny to me.

"Tit happens," I offer, and then the laugh I'm trying to hold in bursts out of me like machine gun fire because I totally meant to say *it happens*. A smile sneaks over Sutton's face, and he chuckles, although I can tell he's trying not to. I extend my hand to him. "I'm Falon," I introduce myself, and Sutton just stares at my waiting palm. "You're supposed to shake it," I explain, and his eyes move from my hand back up to my face.

"Why?" he asks, curious, and I chuckle.

"Honestly, I have no idea," I admit. "Where I come from, people do it when they first meet."

Sutton reaches out and grabs my wrist with his big meaty hand and proceeds to move my whole arm until my hand is shaking. I watch my hand flip flopping all over the place like a fish on a hook, and I realize that technically he is doing what I said he's supposed to do. I crack up when he stops and then offers me his hand to shake. I don't know why, but I do to his arm exactly what he just did to mine instead of showing him what a handshake is really supposed to be. Maybe it has something to do with the weight that lifts from my soul as I laugh and reinvent the handshake with him. Or maybe I'm just a fucking weirdo; either way, I feel safe and hopeful for the first time since I woke up in this strange place.

"Alright, Sutton, let's make me a terminator," I announce when our hand shaking is done. He looks at me, perplexed, and I slap his rock hard pec twice in encouragement. "I'll explain later."

Sutton nods at me and then a devilish smile takes over his face. "Let's begin."

10

"No, Falon!" Sutton bellows and comes stomping toward me. "You're not feeling the counter attack!" he tells me for the four thousandth time.

I rub at my ribs and glare at him. "I promise you I am most definitely feeling the counter attack," I argue, my irritation clear. I'm practically one big fucking bruise at this point, and I've yet to get a hit in. Sarai, my opponent, gives me a sweet smile, and I fight the urge to chuck my sword at her. My ego is probably more bruised at this point than my body, and that's fucking saying something.

"You should *feel* the shift in the air when she changes her stance or the direction of a hit. You should feel it coming as easily as the air current through your feathers when you fly. You're not tapping into your instincts. You're not *one* inside," Sutton explains once again, his closed fist hitting his chest at the end of his statement.

"I know that!" I shout, exasperation dripping from my words. "My gryphon is an asshole! I keep telling you that. She won't even wake up to help me best a thirteen-year-old." I gesture to Sarai who is momentarily distracted by something that looks like a dragonfly whizzing through the air.

Sutton's gaze fills with sympathy, and he steps closer to me. "Don't be so hard on yourself. Sarai's the best with weapons I've ever seen, but you're ready to learn from her. You've worked hard these past three weeks, you just need to figure out how to work with your animal at all times, or you'll never get anywhere in the next phase of training."

I look past him to the part of the field where shifted gryphons are learning to defend and attack. I exhale a deep resigned breath.

"I can't make her listen to me, Sutton. She doesn't even wake up when I *actually* need her. She's a lazy, good for nothing gryphon who likes to pump me full of hormones to fuck with me and then gets off on leaving me hanging at all other times."

I leave off that she sits up at attention whenever Zeph or Ryn are nearby, as it feels like TMI. I barely see them these days anyway, between training and working on my project for Tysa, which means my bitch of a gryphon is pretty much dormant at all times.

My trade with Tysa has worked out well. I now own several pairs of pants and shirts, a couple bra-like garments I walked Tysa through making, and last week, she gifted me with my very own braided armor vest and pants. What looked like leather turned out to be something called Narwagh hide. I guess it's like a pig or something. The material is protective on the outside but soft and somewhat stretchy against my skin. The pants she made are so badass they almost look like black scales all over my legs, and I laughed so hard when I saw them.

The story of what I thought I was when I woke up flying in the sky that first time, slipped out one night when I was working late at Tysa's house. She and her mate, Moro, laughed so hard they had tears streaming down their face, and now I have black dragon scale-looking Narwagh armor. Tysa is the fucking best, and aside from Sutton, my only friend here. The looks of mistrust and disdain from people are still a daily occurrence, but mostly they just ignore me now, which I suppose is a step in the right direction.

Sutton snaps his fingers in front of my face a couple of times. "Focus, Falon, you're as bad as Sarai sometimes with daydreaming and distractions."

I offer him a sheepish look, and he chuckles and reaches out and tucks a wayward strand of ghost-white hair behind my ear. He's been doing that a lot lately, touching me or looking at me softly. I'm not sure how to take it. Is he expressing attraction, or is this just how he is? I honestly have no fucking clue what to think about any of it. Sutton is handsome and nice. He's an incredible teacher, and I like talking to him, but I don't know if there's more beyond that.

"Ami!" Sutton bellows out of nowhere, and I jump from the shock of his sudden booming beckon. "I'm going to have you pair off with Ami for a while. He struggled with his gryphon too, and I think he can teach you to get past your blocks. You two have some things in common," Sutton tells me cryptically, reaching out and tugging the end of my braid as he walks past to intercept Ami and fill him in on the plan.

I stand there awkwardly like a forgotten kid after school, waiting at the now empty pick up line. Ami looks over at me as Sutton speaks to him, and I almost expect his eyes to go white as he observes me, like they did when Zeph brought him into my first interrogation. Ami gives Sutton a nod and then makes his way over to me. He's just slightly taller than me, lean, and from the look of him, still growing into his body. He shakes Bieber-brown hair out of his face, and his light brown eyes land on mine.

"You won't need that," he tells me, his chin jerking toward the wooden sword still gripped in my hand. "Follow me," he instructs, and then he turns and walks toward the bordering trees. I turn back and look for Sutton like I need his reassurance that this is okay, but he's busy working with the other trainees. So I drop my practice sword at my feet and follow the mysterious Ami away from the training fields.

I'm grateful for the boots that Tysa got for me as I follow Ami in silence over rocky terrain and then through a shallow part of the river until we're standing close to the edge of the cliff on the opposite side of the cliff castle. We both stare out into the never-ending water, and I wait for him to tell me what we're doing here. He walks casually to the cliff's edge, and I tense. He sits down and hangs his legs over the rim and motions for me to do the same. I hesitate.

"You afraid of heights?" he teases.

"I always think I'm not until I get somewhere danger-ously high, and then I rethink my answer," I offer as I inch slowly closer to the edge. I move like a baby fawn on shaky legs, arms outstretched like if I trip and go over, somehow my noodle arms will stop me.

"You do have wings, you know," Ami rags, and I shoot him an unamused glare.

"Psshh, pretty sure my gryphon would get a kick out of me falling off this cliff," I inform him, and he chuckles.

"You most likely wouldn't die if you fell," he offers, as if that should be all the reassurance I need.

"Yeah, I've been there and done that thanks to your fear-less leader. I'll take a hard pass on any future bone-crushing falls." I sit carefully next to Ami and hang my legs over the edge like he does. Wind rushes up the cliff side like it's trying to escape the crashing waves below. It carries cool mist on its back, and the breeze flirts around us as we sit and take it all in.

"It's beautiful here," I offer reverently.

"Yeah, something about this place is very calming to people like us," he agrees, and then he pulls his arm back and chucks a pebble over the cliff. It's impossible to track the little rock as it falls to meet the water, but I try anyway.

"People like us?" I query.

"Yeah, you know, highborn, dirty bloods, Ouphe tainted," he sneers. "This place used to belong to the Ouphe. Their magic is practically built into the cliffs themselves. You'll see their writing all over the castle and the surrounding land. I think that's why people with more Ouphe in their blood than Gryphon, people like you and me, resonate so much with this place."

I take a moment to contemplate his words and chuck my own rock into the depths of the water as I do. "So is that how you can do what you can, because you're more Ouphe than Gryphon?" I ask, hoping I'm not crossing some kind of line with my curiosity.

"Yeah, I'm a seer, or at least that's what my mom called it before she..." Ami trails off, and I can tell by his tone and the look on his face that's not a statement that ends well.

"How does it work?" I ask, veering around the *what happened* that sits on my tongue.

"It feels like an extra sense almost, something I can tap into whenever I want, just like I can with my other senses," he explains, and I nod my head in understanding. "When I tap into the sight, I can see colors mostly. Different colors mean different things, and a person's colors can shift and change depending on what they're doing, saying, or how they're feeling."

"Are you glad you can do that?" I ask, and I watch his face as he thinks about my question.

"I don't like or dislike it, it just is. I've always been like this. I don't know any other way," he tells me matter-of-factly.

We fall into an awkward silence as Ami goes full Yoda mic drop on me, and I sit there and process his *it just is* attitude. After a minute or so, the drive to either move or talk has me opening my mouth again.

"So Sutton said you also had issues with your gryphon; was yours a lazy pigeon, too?" I ask, trying to make the question light and ignoring the undertone of tension that reverberates in my words.

Ami nods and releases a humorless chuckle. "Sutton will tell you that you need to be one with your animal because you are one. There is no *us* and *them*. We're the same being inside when we're in both forms, but it never felt that way for me. Maybe I just relate to my animal differently, or maybe for us it actually is different. It's possible that for us, we are separate beings from our gryphons because we have more than one natural strain of magic pumping through our veins."

"So if I can't be one with her like Sutton is saying, how do I make this work?" I ask, gesturing to my body and the dormant gryphon getting plenty of beauty sleep inside of me.

"Your animal was locked away for how long?" Ami asks me.

"I'm twenty-five, and I just shifted for the first time almost four weeks ago. I mean, I could feel her before, more than I can now anyway, but I could never shift," I explain.

"What changed to make her shift now?" he queries, curiosity clear in his tone.

"I'm not one hundred percent sure, but I suspect that my grandmother gave me a ring that kept me from shifting. It also made me look different. I never had the white hair and the lavender eyes until after it was destroyed and I woke up here," I add.

Ami runs his gaze over my white locks for a second before bringing his light brown eyes back to mine. "What about your parents?"

"They died when I was five; I was raised by my grandmother." I can see the question he's about to ask, and I answer it before it can escape his eyes and fall out of his mouth. "She knew what I was. She had to. I suspect that she was a gryphon too, but I have no idea why she wouldn't tell me the truth. She obviously sent me to that gate for a reason. Maybe she knew this would happen, maybe she didn't, but I'm left trying to piece it all together."

Ami nods in understanding and pulls his gaze from mine to look out over the water. I reach back, ready to eject another pebble out into the dark depths of the massive lake when suddenly, out of nowhere, I feel Ami's hands slam hard against my back as he pushes me off the cliff.

I know without any shadow of a doubt that I have the last three weeks of training to thank for my now quick as lightning reflexes. They don't stop me from going over, but they do help me to reach back and grab Ami's forearm, which is the reason I'm slamming into the hard dirt and rock of the cliff instead of tumbling down into the crashing waves a couple hundred feet below. I grab onto the meat of Ami's arm with everything that I have in me as I bounce back from the side of the cliff and proceed to dangle in the air. My weight pulls Ami forward, and it looks like all it would take is an angry breeze to send him toppling over me.

"What the fuck are you doing?" I scream at him.

My yell bounces back at me and dislodges a couple of rocks from the cliff face. They clunk ominously down the steep rocky ledge. Terror pulls at me, and I look up into Ami's calm light brown eyes. My ability to judge a person's character is clearly fucking broken. I did not pick up on any psycho vibes from this kid until now.

"I know this probably seems abrupt, Falon, but I promise you this is the best way. Your gryphon won't let you die, and you have to force her hand," Ami yells down at me, his voice lacking any of the panic and fear that mine has.

I scream bloody murder and struggle as Ami starts to peel the fingers of one of my hands off of his arm. "Please stop, don't do that," I beg as I try to tighten my tiring grip. "Ami, my gryphon doesn't work that way. She doesn't wake up when I'm scared or I'm falling," I yell at him.

"Oh you won't just be falling, I'll be attacking you while you do," Ami tells me matter-of-factly, and then his eyes change from light brown into the white and black of an eagle's eyes. Something sharp stings my forearm, and I watch as talons start to pierce my skin from the tips of Ami's fingers. A growl bubbles up out of his throat, and my blood speckles my face as I thrash, both wanting to get away from him and not knowing what will happen to me if I let go. There's a chance Ami is right and somehow my gryphon will step in to save my ass. But there's also a chance that won't happen. It certainly hasn't so far.

"Ami!" I scream in protest as talons dig deeper into my arm, and I watch helplessly as he slowly starts to shift.

"What are you doing?" roars through the air. Zeph flies up at Ami's back and lands with a thud I can see vibrate through the rocks around me.

His honey eyes are livid as they meet my terrified gaze, and his black wings give an angry snap as he stomps toward us. Fury pours off of him as Ami turns to Zeph and growls a menace filled warning. And for some reason, *that* of all things punches my lazy pigeon of a gryphon right in the face, and she tears awake inside of me. I scream as the shift flashes through me, ripping me apart to make room for her.

I've never been awake for a shift before, and it hurts a hell of a lot more than Gran ever told me it would.

"Don't fight her," Ami yells at me, and then my body goes weightless as he strips my grip from him, and I start to fall.

11

I'm sucked into myself, aware but not in control. It's like I'm sitting in someone else's body watching them run the show. A screech pours out of my razor sharp beak, and then I'm no longer falling but unfurling massive black wings and demanding the air take me where I want to go. My panic is lost amidst all the new sensations. I can feel and taste the wind. My vision is sharper but more limited in a way I can't quite grasp.

"Pigeon?" I ask tentatively, aware that some other consciousness is flying me out over the water. I can feel in our muscles that we're going to turn back, and a determination fills me as we angle toward where Ami and Zeph were standing on the cliff. Just as we do, a large black gryphon dives off of the tall rocky ledge, and a thrill of excitement sounds off inside of me. I'm pretty sure that's solely the Pigeon's feelings about the massive gryphon streaking through the air toward us, because all I can seem to do is fight the flashbacks of being attacked by said asshole gryphon and what happened after.

My gryphon cuts hard to the right, away from Zeph, and we pick up speed. I'm not sure how I know, but she wants him to chase her, and as weird as I think that is, I light up with giddy satisfaction as we speed over the water in our best efforts to break the sound barrier.

"Fuck yeah, Pigeon," I hoot in encouragement as she shows me just what we're capable of. We move like lightning through the air, and certainty that *this* is what we're meant for whips through me and fills me with freedom and happiness.

I can feel her preen with my appreciation, and I laugh, which creates this odd chuffing sound in my chest. It's like my gryphon and I are separate and yet also the same. I'm not sure how to wrap my mind around it, but I can feel her independently from me, and yet we both have the ability to control the same body. I'm tempted to see just what I can do with these wings, but an image of my hand being slapped like a naughty toddler about to touch something dangerous flashes in my mind.

"Did you just...?" I trail off for a second. *"Pigeon, can you talk to me?"* I ask her in awe, and I swear to fuck I can feel her roll her eyes. My shocked and manic laugh fills my head, and that strange little chuffing sound starts up again in my chest. I can't lie, gryphon laughter is fucking adorable. I suddenly feel bad for all the names I've called her and just how pissed I've been. Then I remember exactly why I've been so pissed, and the frustration comes surging back.

"If you can hear me and talk to me, where the hell have you been this whole time?" I demand. *"I've needed you,"* I add, neither of us missing the hurt that tints that thought. A flash of my mother's ring pops up in my mind. It's replaced by an image of our reflection in the water, and then I'm overwhelmed by the pain we felt when we smashed into the ground.

"You were hurt?" I ask, as it dawns on me that just because I seemed to escape that whole crash unscathed, it

and I can practically hear the splat as I crash into it. One of my wings crunches against the smooth trunk of the tree on impact, and an audible snap rings through me. If I had air in my lungs, I would scream from the pain. I slide down unceremoniously to the base of the tree and gasp for breath. My lungs fill, but I quickly realize what a mistake it is to try to breathe too deeply, as a stabbing pain shoots through my chest. I pant through the agony, certain my ribs are broken, my shoulder is fucked up, and I'm pretty sure I broke a wing.

I lie with my cheek pressed against the cool dirt cocooning the roots of the tree and blink through the shock and hurt. I really need to figure out this whole landing thing, because I'm over the smash and stop I seem to be doing all the time. Bare feet tromp into my line of sight, but when I try to lift my head to see who it is, agony shoots through my neck, shoulder, and wing. I rest my head back where it was, content to let the mystery of the owner of the feet remain a little longer.

"Falon, can you hear me?" Zeph asks, panic bleeding out of his voice, and he drops down in front of me. "Be okay, be okay," I think I hear him whisper chant, but it's hard to be sure through the ringing in my ears.

Zeph brushes my hair out of my face, and I get a clear line of sight to the huge cock hanging between his crouched thighs. I stare at it shamelessly for a couple of seconds, the soft shaft dangling from a nest of black curls, and I have the sudden urge to see if it feels as squishy as it looks. Since blinking is about the only movement that doesn't hurt right now, I'm forced to keep my hands to myself.

"Little sparrow, can you hear me?" Zeph asks again, leaning down closer to my face.

"Your telephone pole dick is staring at me," I croak, and I swear the thing twitches.

"Where are you hurt?" he demands, his voice abandoning the tenderness that was just there and falling back into familiar gruff territory.

"Everywhere," I announce, but it sounds like a question.

"Rutting centaurs!" he exclaims, and it sounds like he's swearing, but I have no idea what he just said. "I'm going to have to set your wing before it heals wrong and I have to rebreak it to fix it."

I don't respond in any way.

"Here's the thing, little sparrow, you can't scream. The forest isn't safe on this side of the lake, and too much noise will bring a rut load of trouble down on our heads."

Once more, I don't say or do anything, and Zeph grows quiet. "Cum on a tree sprite," he swears again, and I don't know what he's doing, but it's making Heavy D and The Boys bounce around. I feel two large hands lift me up by the shoulders, and a shriek of protest pours out of me.

"Shhh, you *have* to be quiet," he scolds me, but I fucking can't.

Tears stream down my face as he picks me up and pulls me into his lap. His body is warm against my chilled skin, but every jostle feels like torture, and I scream through gritted teeth as he rests my head against his chest. He finally has a clear view of my left shoulder, and he swears again.

"Your shoulder's out, too," he informs me, his tone clinical, and I whimper and pant through the new wave of pain crashing through me from being moved. "Little sparrow, I know it hurts, but you have to be quiet. If they find us, we'll be tortured and killed."

I'm not sure who the *they* are he's talking about, but the worry in his tone has me gritting my teeth and nodding my head. I turn my face into his heated skin and squeeze my eyes closed in anticipation. I'm not sure how much time goes by, but he doesn't immediately reset my shoulder or wing like I expected. I relax slightly, and that's when he thrusts my elbow up, and my shoulder pops back into place. The cry I can't swallow back down is muffled against his skin. He doesn't even give me time to catch my breath before his hands are on my wing, snapping things back into place and causing an inferno of anguish to blaze through me.

My vision tunnels, and I beg for unconsciousness. Just when I get a grip on the blackness and try to pull it over me like a comforting blanket, it slips from my grasp, and I'm left panting against Zeph's chest. Pain laps through me, cresting and falling. My tears drip down my cheek and speckle his olive toned skin.

"Shhhh, little sparrow, it's over. You did well. It's okay," Zeph coos at me as he wipes the tears from my face with his calloused thumb.

His rough fingertips feel oddly soothing, and a shuddering breath moves through me as I try to stem my tears. His hand moves from my face momentarily, and he runs it up my spine to the base of my neck. Familiar tingles move through the muscles in my back, and my wings fold up inside of me again, taking some of the pain with them. I gasp in momentary relief, and my eyes fly open. Zeph's honey-eyed gaze is fixed on my face, and I stare into his stunning eyes, suddenly very captivated.

Short black lashes frame his intense stare as it drops from my eyes to my lips. I'm very aware that we're both naked, but instead of being uncomfortable with that fact, I have to admit that I like it. Satisfaction hums through me, and I know I have Pigeon to thank for it, but beneath her contentedness, *I* also feel safe and glad to be in his arms. My eyes drop to his lips momentarily before they snake back up his gorgeous face. Heat unfurls in my core, and I feel him hardening against my hip, his length rising to skim both of my ass cheeks. When my gaze meets his again, I'm surprised by the desire I see floating in the thick honey hue of his eyes.

An image of me sitting up and straddling his lap pops up in my mind. I watch as I brush my mouth teasingly against his lips, pulling back a little as he leans in for a kiss. I want to watch his face as I slowly lower myself down on his cock. The tip of him easily parts my wet lips, and I moan as he starts to fill me up. Zeph growls, and I smile as I lift myself up, not letting him go any deeper inside of me. I roll my hips and bounce in his lap so that just the tip of him works in and out of me. I'm eagerly awaiting the moment that he gets fed up with just the tip of his dick getting wet and takes control, slamming his hips up hard and burying his delicious cock deep inside of me.

A distant screech pulls me from my naughty daydream, and Zeph's heated gaze flashes up from mine to the sky. He searches for something, and I feel his body shifting from need to action. *Why am I disappointed by that? I don't even like this guy.* Yes, I got a little swoony as he fixed me and gave me some petting, but he's also the reason I was fucked up in the first place. Zeph rises suddenly from his crouch and starts moving swiftly through the forest. I bite down against the pain that strikes through me at the jostling of my arm, and hope that my shifter genes kick in soon and start healing me.

Zeph moves from tree to tree, his eyes darting from the path he's tracking through the forest up to the sky, checking for whatever threat he's anticipating. I stay quiet, not wanting to distract him or do anything that could clue whatever is hunting us in on our location. Another screech fills the air, this one closer, and Zeph's muscles tense as he freezes under a canopy of branches and needles. He holds me bridal style, and his grip tightens as he turns and presses me against the tree. The bark against my slowly healing shoulder fucking hurts, and a whimper I can't help sneaks out from my lips.

"Shhhhh," Zeph's deep whisper brushes over my face, his mouth a hair's breadth away from mine. His gaze goes distant, and I can tell he's listening for something as our breaths mingle and the drive to kiss him bubbles up inside of me.

"Not the time or the place, Pigeon," I scold. *"Your bullshit has caused enough trouble already,"* I add, and then I wet my lips with my tongue and try to ignore the fact that if I just leaned in a little, I could claim his full lips as mine.

After a couple beats of silence, Zeph starts to move again, but the erection slapping against my ass as we run makes me horny as fuck and aware that Zeph is not unaffected by my naked body in his arms. *Maybe I'm not as indifferent as I thought to this asshole. Or maybe I just need to get laid, and the position we find ourselves in would make anyone start to think dirty thoughts.* I latch onto the second explanation, much to Pigeon's dismay, but it has to be that. I know she's attracted to him on some instinctual level, but on a logical level, I am not.

He's a dick, and I can't just excuse that because he happens to have a pretty one I would like to play with right now. We just need to make it through this fucked up episode of *Naked and Afraid*, and then I'll find some other pretty dick to play with. A growl rumbles in Zeph's chest, and I look up in alarm to see what set him off. I search the sky like he's been doing, but I don't see or sense anything. My eyes dart to Zeph's, and his stare is fixed on me. He's angry, and his hold tightens on me. I wiggle uncomfortably until he stops squeezing me, and he looks away, irritation and fury in his eyes.

Yep, definitely need to start hunting for a pretty dick attached to a nice gryphon who's down for a little no strings attached fuckery, I decide, and I stop myself from nestling into Zeph's chest the way Pigeon wants me to as he starts running again.

12

"What is this place?" I ask, not able to help it as I'm carried deeper into a cave of red rock with black veins crawling through it.

"It's a hidden shelter. We have them scattered around for situations just like this," Zeph tells me as he makes his way further in.

Our voices crash against the rock and bounce back at us, but Zeph is talking, so I figure it's safe to keep doing the same.

"And what exactly is it that we're running from?" I press. He said it wasn't safe on this side of the lake, but I still have no idea what's going on.

"The Avowed patrol this side of the lake. It's the furthest their territory reaches. You could have been spotted any minute, which is why I—"

"Made me crash," I interrupt, and he narrows his gaze at me.

"Saved your life," he corrects, and then he sets me on a cold rock and hurries away from me like I have something contagious.

"Saved my life, almost killed me, potato, po-tah-to," I

snark as I stand up in an effort to save my ass cheeks from frostbite.

Fuck, it's cold in here. I fold my arms over my diamond hard nipples and try to rein in the teeth chattering that's started. Zeph pulls wood from a massive stack toward the back of the cave and has a fire flickering to life in a matter of minutes. I step closer to it and try not to be mesmerized by the fire shadows now dancing over Zeph's massive and well-muscled body. He bends over a large wooden chest that's been situated against a wall of the cave and starts to rummage through it.

I tilt my head in appreciation. Fabric smacks me in the face, and it jerks me away from the pervy thoughts starting to rise up in my mind. Maybe if I fucked him once, it would get it out of my system? The eager head nod I can practically feel Pigeon giving me makes me suddenly leery of that thought. I hold up the bunched, dark green fabric in my hands to find a large long-sleeved shirt. I pull it over my head, ignoring the musty smell, and it falls just shy of the tops of my knees. The laces that cinch up the neck dip down to my naval, and I start pulling the leather ties tighter and covering up. I roll up the sleeves until I can find my hands, and by the time I'm done making the large shirt fit, I find Zeph in a pair of too short and too tight pants.

I can see the outline of his cock a third of the way down his left thigh, and I'm not sure which is worse, staring directly at it or at the hint of it now in his pants. *How about you don't look at it at all, Falon? That just might help the too horny for your own good situation you've got going on right now.* I nod in agreement with my internal scolding and lift my eyes up from Zeph's dick, vowing that my gaze will be waist high for the rest of this fucked up adventure.

I roll my shoulder, relieved to find that it's only a little sore now, and I poke at my ribs and breathe in deeply when

I discover that they're at the same stage of healing. I should be all patched up by morning. Zeph shakes out some kind of fur and lays it on the ground next to the fire. He shakes out another one and then tosses it to me, and I mirror his actions on my side of the fire. *I guess we're back to trying to stay as far away from each other as we can.* I ignore the irritation that surges through me with that thought.

I sit down on the soft fur and run my hands through it. I thought it was black at first, but now that I'm closer, I can see that it's blue. I open my mouth to ask what kind of animal this came from and look up just in time to catch a waterskin that's about to hit me in the face. I stop its punishing trajectory and snatch it out of the air.

"Watch it!" I chide with a glare aimed at Zeph's back. Is there some invisible line now that he can't cross to hand me things? He has to chuck them willy nilly at me without any fucking warning?

"What's your fucking problem?" I ask as I set the waterskin down beside me.

Zeph turns a loathsome glare on me. "*You* are my fucking problem," he snaps at me, his mouth stumbling over the word fucking, like he's never said it before.

I stand up defensively and take a step toward him. "What the hell did I do?" I demand, fed up with all the unearned hostility that's been rolling off of him since we stepped into this cave.

"We're in this situation because of you. I'm at risk, which means my people are at risk, all because of *you*." His words are coated in venom as he spits them out and steps toward me.

I close the distance between us, pressing my chest against his and rise up on my tiptoes. It only brings my eye level higher up on his chest, but it makes me feel more powerful all the same. "We're here because one of your people threw me off a cliff. No one has told me where it's safe to fly. My gryphon didn't know any better. Maybe if you stopped treating me like the spy you know I'm not, I would have fucking known what's safe and what's off limits."

"You have no business being here," he shouts down into my face.

"Then let me fucking go home!" I scream back at him. "You think I want to be here with you? You think I like being looked at by everyone like I'm shit on their shoe, being ignored, ridiculed, made to feel responsible for something I didn't even do? I have white fucking hair, but I am *not* Avowed. I know shit-all about your fucking war. You're the asshole that brought me here. You're the asshole not letting me leave!"

"I have no choice!" he bellows, his eyes filled with anger.

"Well, I fucking do," I seethe at him, and then I head for the opening of the cave.

"Where do you think you're going?"

"Away! You don't want me here, I don't want to be here, problem solved," I throw over my shoulder.

"They will find you," Zeph threatens, the words ricocheting off the *give no fucks* armor I just wrapped myself in.

"Maybe." I shrug, ignoring the twinge of pain it sets off in my shoulder. "If I get caught, I'll deal with them; if not, I'll find my own way home."

I stomp toward the waning light at the entrance of the cave. It's clear the sun is going down, and the rational side of me argues that setting off into strange and unfamiliar territory right before it gets dark might not be the best plan of action. I ignore the self-preservation instinct and opt to focus on my need to get the fuck out of here. I've had enough with all of this shit. It was fun to train and figure out what I was while it lasted, but I have a life to get back to, and Zeph is right, I have no business being here.

I'm pulled back suddenly and pushed against the red and black wall of the cave. Zeph cages me in with both of his arms on either side of my head and presses his mountain of a body into mine.

"You will stay right here," he orders on a growl.

"Get the fuck off me, asshole, who the hell do you think you are?" I shout at him as I try my hardest to shove him off of me.

"They will catch you," he repeats, like somehow it should explain everything.

"Why do you fucking care?" I challenge.

My lavender gaze, filled with fire and hurt, slams up against his melted honey stare that's leaking frustration and fury.

"They would hurt you, force the mark on you," he tells me, his voice smooth and even, his eyes suddenly begging mine to understand. "I can't let that happen," he confesses, and then he shocks the hell out of me by pressing even closer and leaning down to run the tip of his nose up the bridge of mine.

I breathe in, surprised, and my lungs fill with his scent. It taints my anger and indignation with something I don't understand. I feel the need to soothe him. To fuck him. To fight him. I'm bewildered by the onslaught of conflicting needs and emotions. His lips are so close. Our breaths are ragged. His chest is pressing against mine, each lungful of air stroking my nipples and lighting up my body. I lift my hands, needing to touch him, but I force the traitorous limbs down and ball my fists at my side.

Zeph drops his face to the crook of my shoulder and inhales deeply. His muscles relax minutely and then tense again. The tip of his nose runs up the side of my neck, and he breathes me in, his lips barely skimming my heated skin.

"Just stay here where it's safe, little sparrow, and when we get back, I will take you home," he rumbles into my ear.

My body responds to his tone, and need pools between my thighs, but my brain responds to his words. He's going to send me away. Zeph steps back from me, taking all my warmth with him, and walks toward the dusk-kissed entrance of the cave.

"I'm going to find some food. Stay here. I promise I will get you home just as soon as I can." With that, he disappears, and I'm left panting and confused, clutching the rock of the wall I'm still pressed against.

I clench my thighs against my body's demand for satiation, but inside I feel crushed. Even Pigeon is fucking sad, and that feels beyond wrong to me. *"I'm sorry,"* I offer her uselessly, and she retreats further inside of me. I debate for a minute what I should do. Part of me is tempted to leave anyway, but the other part doesn't want to risk capture. If the Avowed are as bad as the Hidden say, it would just make things worse for me. I want to go home, and Zeph said he'll get me there. I decide I can put up with his hatred a little longer if I get what I want in the end.

I feel a sliver of hope from Pigeon that maybe Zeph will come around, but I do everything I can to keep my thoughts on that to myself. Once an asshole, always an asshole, and we deserve more than that. I push off from the rocky wall and head back toward my fur and the warm fire. I take a drink from the waterskin and moan as the clean, cool water fills my mouth. It tastes like heaven, and I try not to drink too much, not knowing how long this water needs to last.

My moan echoes off the rock and dances around me. The sound teases my thoughts, and I find myself replaying my naughty daydream from earlier when I was in Zeph's arms. Sensations flutter down to my clit, and I shake my head at myself. *Get a fucking grip, Falon.* I lie back with an exasperated sigh, but the feel of the hem of my shirt brushing against my thighs brings my salacious thoughts back to the forefront. *Fuck that gryphon asshole for leaving me so needy.* Pigeon rears up in agreement, and I moan again in complaint against how horny I am.

I'm just taking the edge off, I tell myself as I bring one hand up to pinch my nipple and dip the other hand between my thighs. *Better to get myself off than throw myself at someone who doesn't want me.* I spread my lips, not at all surprised to feel how drenched I am, and dip two fingers inside of me. I moan again as I pull my wet need up to my clit and start circling it. I move my hand to my other nipple and pinch it hard as I play with myself. It doesn't take long for the pressure to build inside of me. I grind against my own hand and pull my fingers away from my clit and dip them back inside. I pick up the pace, the base of my palm hitting my clit as I thrust my fingers in and out, stroking all the spots I like.

I come on a deep moan and work myself quickly into another orgasm, forcing the sensations to smash together and prolonging the intensity. I writhe and ride my orgasm like a wave, reveling in the delicious tingles that ripple through my body as I float down through the pleasure. I release a deep contented exhale and stroke my fingers in a circle one last time inside of me before I pull out.

That was exactly what I needed.

Solo orgasms are never quite as good as orgasms other people pull from my body, but I'll take what I can get at this point. Need no longer drives my every thought, and my mind feels clearer now. I rinse my hand with a little bit of water and pull my shirt back down. I lie on my side and stare at the flames of the fire, letting them fight off the cold that's pressing in against me.

The crackling of the fire echoes around the cave, and strange noises press in on the darkening solace surrounding me. It sounds like some animal or insect's song and makes me think of the way crickets chirp at night back home. I'm once again reminded of my stranger status in this completely foreign land, and loneliness bubbles up inside of me.

My gran's face rises to the surface of my thoughts, but I bat it away. I'm not past the lies and subterfuge enough to embrace any fond memories and longing that accompanies stray thoughts of her. I try and fail to look through the cracks of our history, to read between the lines of our relationship to discover why she kept all of this from me, but I come up with nothing. My mind wanders to my mom and dad, their smiles, the sound of their laughter, and I let the loneliness I often try to ignore take up temporary residence in my chest for a while.

I'm not sure how long I lie there, staring at the fire, trying to sift through my past, but the sound of Zeph stomping back into the cave pulls me away from my thoughts. He freezes just as he comes into view, and I sit up concerned. His nostrils flare, and his gaze moves from me as he scans the cave. I'm not sure what he's looking for, and I turn, confused, and look around the cave too.

"What happened in here?" he asks, and I watch as his nostrils flare again. His pupils look like they dilate, but that could just be from the now dark cave and the dim light the fire is providing.

"What do you mean?" I ask, breathing in deeply myself, in an effort to identify whatever it is that he's smelling. It suddenly dawns on me what he must be scenting. I feel my cheeks heat, and I shrug, hoping it looks nonchalant.

"Uh...I was just...um...entertaining myself." My statement sounds more like a question, and my gaze darts away from Zeph's for a second and then darts back. *Don't look at his crotch, Falon! Keep those eyes above the waist!* Zeph looks pained for a beat, and then his stare fills up with familiar frustration. He stomps past me, chucking something large and turquoise in my direction. I catch it with both hands and focus on it, ignoring Zeph as he huffs and puffs while settling himself on his own fur.

I rotate the football shape in my hands and suddenly recognize it as the yummy fruit Tysa got for me the morning of the alarms. I look up just in time to see Zeph crack his fruit over his knee and slurp a huge bite out of one half. My stomach rumbles, and I mimic his actions. I hold the bumpy fruit up high and bring it down hard on my knee.

"Motherfucker!" I shout as the only thing that feels like it breaks is my damn knee cap. I drop the fruit and grab onto my knee, rocking back and forth as I grunt in pain.

"What the rut did you do now?" Zeph accuses as he rushes to my side. He tries to move my hands, and I slap his big asshole-ish mitts away.

"Fuck off, I can take care of myself," I snap at him, and he narrows his eyes at me.

"Clearly," he snarks, matching me glare for glare as he trundles back over to his side of the fire.

I look around the cave for a rock and spot the perfect one. I hobble to my feet and grab the fruit. I limp over to the rock and smash the turquoise football fruit on its edge. I release a battle cry of triumph as my fruit splits open, and do a victory dance back to my fur. I catch Zeph watching me, and I shoot him an *I told you so* with my eyes as I bite into the inside of my fruit. The same delicious pineapple and strawberry taste fills my mouth, and I have to slurp up the juice to keep it from making a mess of my face.

"What is this called?" I ask before I slurp and bite into it again.

"Duda fruit," Zeph answers flatly, digging into his own meal and going back to ignoring me.

"It tastes like pineapple to me. Do you guys have that fruit here?" I ask. He doesn't say anything. "I used to hate pineapple when I was younger. That just seems funny to me because now I'm obsessed with it. My gran used to get it on pizza, and I would always pick it off. Holy shit!" I exclaim suddenly, looking down at the turquoise fruit in my hands.

"What?" Zeph demands, rising to come to me and searching around me for whatever has me so stunned.

"She called it dude pizza," I inform him quietly. "I thought it was like a joke about surfers or something, but she was talking about this fruit." I look up at Zeph and take in his face as the fire's light flickers over his features. "She was missing this." I hold up the fruit and stare at it with new understanding.

"What about the rest of your family; did they ever talk about anything that might give you a clue where they come from?"

I think back and try to look at my few memories of my mother and father, but nothing stands out. "My father was from an island. I don't remember the name, and my gran hated talking about it."

"What was *his* name?" Zeph asks, his focus on the wall of the cave and not on me.

"Awlon...Awlon Umbra. He had black hair and lime green eyes that always lit up when he saw me," I tell him, a small smile sneaking across my face at the memory.

"Awlon the Dark was the last reigning prince of the Ouphe," Zeph announces, and he looks at me with even more scrutiny than he did before. "He died though, he was murdered by a servant," he adds, and he sounds like he's trying to convince himself of these facts. "Your mother?"

"Noor. Her name was Noor." I try to recall her maiden name, but it doesn't come to me. I know it was different than Gran's, but I can't remember what it was.

Zeph gasps and then starts to cough. My gaze flashes up to his, and I can't tell if he's choking on something or trying to cover up his reaction to my mother's name.

"What?" I demand, handing him the waterskin.

He takes a deep pull, and I wait impatiently for him to explain what sent him into a coughing fit. He shakes his head at me as he swallows another mouthful of water. "The name Noor is common around these parts. You'd have to check the archives with her full name to see if you have any other family here," he finally explains, and I sag with disappointment. "We should sleep; we have a long walk ahead of us tomorrow, and we both need to heal."

I nod at Zeph's retreating back and watch him settle on his side of the fire, his back to me. I can't shake the suspicion that he's not being straight with me. Then again, it's not like I've been in the loop about anything since I got here. I finish the rest of my meal and wash the sticky juice from my hands and face with some water from the skin. I lie on my side again and scoot closer to the fire, feeling cold. It's like the elements and my memories are working in tandem to make me feel empty and freezing.

I debate for a second about scooting even closer to the stone ringed fire pit, but the image of me rolling into the fire in my sleep keeps me from closing the distance. A shiver runs through me, and I pull as much of the fur around me as I can while still lying on it. Zeph releases an irritated huff.

"I can hear your teeth chattering from here," he observes, annoyance painting every word.

I flip his back the bird and try to stop my sudden shivering. *"Psst...Pigeon,"* I call. *"Want to go all feathered and save me from hypothermia?"* I ask, but she doesn't stir. *"Who's a pretty gryphon?"* I say in my most playful voice usually reserved for cute puppies and kittens. Nothing. *"Fine, but if I die in my sleep from the cold, you only have yourself to blame,"* I warn her.

I pull the top of my shirt over my mouth and try to breathe warm air into the makeshift cocoon. Zeph grumbles and stands up, grabs his fur, and tromps over to my side of the fire. He lies down, his back touching mine, and silence fills the cave again. After a while of lying with Zeph at my back, I start to warm up. Apparently, he's an asshole and a walking, talking space heater, who knew? I snuggle into my furs, my shivers chased away by his close proximity, and I fall asleep to the memory of my dad's happy-to-see-me eyes.

13

"**F**ucking, fuck, fucker!" I whisper growl at the stick that just tried to stab through the soft arch of my foot.

Zeph shoots me a warning look that tells me to keep it down, so I proceed to pick up said fucking stick and chuck it at him. I nail him in the back of the head, and the stick clings to his curly hair. I raise my hands triumphantly and mouth *score*! I give myself a thousand points for nailing him exactly where I wanted to and smile until I step on a rock which then finds itself on the receiving end of my whispered wrath.

I want my fucking shoes and pants. I shifted with them on which means they're probably shredded and sitting at the bottom of the lake, so as soon as we get back, I'm tracking down Ami and making him get me new ones. Tricky little fucker. I'm also going to treat him to a solid junk punch. I should feel wrong about hitting a teenage boy in the junk, but it's the best punishment I can come up with at the moment.

We've been walking all day. I woke up cold and alone in the cave just as the sun was peeking over the horizon. Zeph showed up about ten minutes later with more duda fruit and a side of extra surly gryphon. He said we couldn't take the furs as they would be needed by the next gryphon who sought sanctuary, but he did keep his pants and let me keep my shirt.

"If you would let me carry you, you could stop cursing the ground every two minutes," Zeph snarls quietly at me.

"I'm healed, and I can walk," I defend, repeating the same argument I used when he tried to pick me up back at the cave.

"Well, you're slow and you're clumsy. This is taking twice as long as it should!"

He reaches out to grab me, and I quickly scramble away from him. The whole skin to skin thing we had going on during yesterday's trek is the last thing I need to happen today. I can't spend all day smelling him and feeling his body against mine. It creates too much of a distraction from the fact that I hate him, and I need to focus on that instead of his muscled back and an ass that I want to bounce quarters off of or bite, I haven't quite decided yet.

Zeph lunges for me, and I bite back a squeal and sprint to get away from him. Pigeon sits up, and I can just picture her clapping with glee. She's finally getting the chase she was so desperate for when she flew the fuck out here and landed us in this trouble yesterday. Zeph growls and charges after me, and I pick up the pace, weaving through trees to escape him. I run full out until my lungs protest and I have to slow down in order to fill them properly.

I look back to see if Zeph's closing the distance behind me, but he's not there. I stop completely, trying to listen over my ragged breaths to the sounds around me. I scan the surrounding forest, certain that at any moment, he's going to pop out from somewhere and scare the shit out of me to teach me a lesson. I dart between trees soundlessly and ignore the excitement I feel over this cat and mouse game we're suddenly playing. I feel eyes on me, and my head swivels back and forth as I search for his honey eyes and huge body amidst tree trunks and bushes.

A twig snaps behind me, and I dart forward in an effort to avoid capture. I risk another look over my shoulder, which of course is when I slam right into his massive chest. An *oomph* slams out of me at the contact, and his bruising grip lands on my shoulders.

"Ow, you're fucking hurting me," I warn, and then I freeze as I look up and discover that it's not Zeph who's holding me at all.

"Now what do we have here?" the gryphon shifter asks, the tips of his fingers digging into the meat of my arms even harder. The telltale lilac-on-the-wind smell fills my nose, but there's a sharp citrusy smell to him too. I struggle and try to get away, but I don't scream, too worried that it might bring more hunters my way. The large man slams me against the trunk of a tree, and my head cracks back against it, making me instantly dizzy. The world around me sways, and I try to blink it back into focus.

"What's a pretty highborn girl doing out here at the edge of civilization?" the man asks me, raking his eyes down my body and slowly back up. He inhales deeply, and his smile grows even creepier. "You do look like a vision of naughtiness if I ever saw one," he tells me lasciviously, dropping one hand down to the hem of my shirt.

I whimper and try to kick him away from me, but he clamps his other hand around my throat and squeezes, stopping the air from reaching my lungs. He lifts me off the ground, and I soundlessly claw at the hand around my throat. "Who would bring such a beauty all the way out here, huh, princess? Who's out here playing with this pretty little cunt of yours?"

He snakes his hand under the bottom of my shirt and slowly, threateningly, moves it up my thigh. His pupils dilate, and fear pounds deafeningly in my head. Rage fills my chest, and I suddenly realize it's not just fear pounding inside of me, it's Pigeon ramming herself against my defenses and begging to be let out. I open the door I didn't even know I had closed, and Pigeon explodes out of me. I embrace the shift as I try to keep from drowning in panic, and it's over in the blink of an eye.

The man pinning me to a tree barely has enough time for his eyes to widen in shock before Pigeon clamps her hooked beak around his head and rips it off. She shreds him with no hesitation or remorse, and I cheer her on from inside our gryphon body. Just when I think the brutality is over, Pigeon squats over the destroyed body and pisses on it. I laugh, shocked by the perfect crudeness of her actions, and then proceed to question my own sanity.

Why the fuck do I find this amusing?

We take a minute to glory in our kill and collect ourselves. Pigeon sniffs at the air and takes off in the direction that I just ran from. Worry fills her thoughts, and she flashes an image of Zeph to me and two shadowed figures. *"Shit. I'm pretty sure that's gryphon-speak for he's been caught."* Pigeon stalks through the forest, and she moves so stealthily that I can't even hear a pine needle bend beneath our paws and talons as we make our way to where we scent Zeph and his captors. I haven't spent much time with my gryphon, but I'm discovering that she has some serious skills. Pigeon flashes an image of our reflection on the water to me, and I chuckle.

"And you're fucking beautiful, too," I agree.

Zeph's scent gets stronger as we get closer to where he's being detained, and we can make out at least two voices. That same unusual hint of citrus mixed with the breezy lilac scent that gryphons have tickles my nose. Why do they smell different?

"Where the rut is Sheridan? He left to take a shit ages ago," a voice complains.

"He'll just have to catch up. We need to get this one back to the city for questioning," a gravellier voice declares, and then I hear a thud and a grunt as the owner of the voice kicks Zeph.

Pigeon completely loses it, and before I can even suggest that we come up with a plan of attack, she's charging through the trees and pouncing on one of Zeph's captors. His surprised scream is cut off as she once again displays her expert decapitating skills. We round on the other guy, ready to shred him to pieces, but he shifts into a massive walnut-colored gryphon in less than a second.

"Shit, Pigeon. He's fucking huge," I warn, like somehow she's incapable of seeing that for herself.

Pigeon puffs up as the big brown gryphon roars at us in warning. I expect her to roar her challenge back, but instead Pigeon pounces, flapping her wings to help propel her forward even faster. The other gryphon doesn't seem prepared for this insane plan of action, and that makes two of us. Pigeon snaps at him, but he jerks away from her razor sharp beak and tries to take his own chunk out of our neck. Pigeon rears back to avoid it and bitch-slaps him with a talon-covered hand.

It knocks him off balance, and we're on him before he can recover. We dig the claws of our hind paws into his back and go to work with our talons and beak. The walnut-colored gryphon swipes at us on his back and then releases a pain-filled bellow as we rip off his ear. We scrape up the side of his face, and I'm pretty sure he loses his right eye in the process. He rears back and pumps his wings to help flip him on top of us.

Our back slams into a massive tree trunk, and I feel a crack run up our shoulder blades. Pain flashes through us, but we ignore it and continue to claw at anything and everything we can. I don't realize right away that the gryphon we're trying to kill exposed his neck to us, but Pigeon does, and she goes right for the opening the big brown gryphon created when he reared back. We claw at his throat with everything we have, snapping at the back of his neck with our beak. Blood is everywhere, and it spurs us on. The big gryphon slams us back into the tree in one last ditch effort to get us off of him and then slouches to the ground.

Pigeon scrambles off of his back and immediately tears out what's left of the walnut gryphon's throat. The blood and life pour out of him, but we don't watch it pool around the still body. Pigeon looks around for Zeph, worried that he hasn't shifted and helped to deal with these guys. We find him tied to a tree by a black rope. He's struggling to free himself, and the rope is cutting into his skin in multiple places, making him bleed. Pigeon makes a purring sound, and Zeph immediately goes still. She walks over to Zeph and drops her head, leaning her forehead against his. He closes his eyes and breathes us in. The exchange is odd to me, and I observe them, transfixed by the interaction.

Pigeon slashes through the rope and hisses as it burns our hand. Zeph looks surprised when the rope falls away, and he quickly unwinds it from around his body and his hands. As soon as he does, he erupts into his gryphon. He flaps his wings at us aggressively, and Pigeon growls at him. He charges us, and it pisses both me and Pigeon off. *"We just saved your ass, you fucker!"* I shout at him, and it comes out as a roar from our mouth.

He lowers his head like he's going to use it as a battering ram, but as his honey-colored eagle eyes land on ours, he skids to a stop. Fire punches through me, and Pigeon and I both scream, scared and in agony. Pressure slams into our chest, and I swear if Zeph just hit us, I'm going to fucking kill him. I try to focus on our surroundings as Pigeon drops to the ground, submitting to the pain. I find Zeph locked in the same struggle we are, and it terrifies me. Did those guys do something to us?

"It's just the call being answered, little sparrow." I hear Zeph's voice clear as day in my head, but it makes no sense.

Beyond the burning sensation working its way through my body, I can sense Pigeon's happiness, which confuses me even more. I try to reach for her satisfaction so I can look at it more closely, but she retreats inside of me, and I can feel the shift working to pull her back inside.

"Pigeon, you fucker, what the hell is going on?" I demand as she pulls away, and her chuckle vibrates through me.

The next thing I know, my cheek is pressed against the ground, and dust plumes at my mouth as I pant through the hurt that's radiating in every cell I possess. I blink, and my surroundings come into focus. I watch unfazed as Zeph's big ass charcoal-colored gryphon fully rips off the head of the walnut-colored gryphon that Pigeon already took care of.

Well, I guess he wasn't as affected by the raging inferno that Pigeon and I just experienced.

My vision blurs, and I work to blink it back into focus. When I do, Zeph's gryphon is inches away from me. He nudges my shoulder until I flip over onto my back. I don't fight him, because it hurts to breathe let alone move. He sniffs at me, his beak warm and smooth against my skin. Goose bumps pebble over me, and he huffs out a breath that blows my hair back from my face.

"I don't know what you did to me, asshole, but as soon as I can move, I'm going to pluck out all of your nose hairs," I threaten, and a familiar chuffing sound radiates from Zeph's chest.

you fucking didn't," I growl back, and Pigeon sits up inside of me, responding to the clear challenge Loa is giving us. My vision shifts, and I feel the tips of my fingers elongate and sharpen. Tingles run up my back, and my wings pop out, breaking Ryn's hold.

"Rutting fairies!" he shouts and tries to get a hold of me again, but I'm already just out of reach and charging Loa. Pigeon preens, satisfied by the hint of fear we see in Loa's gaze before she masks it, but we can still smell it seeping off of her.

"Loa, out!" Ryn roars as Zeph slams into me, keeping me from connecting with Loa. I snap at him and watch as Loa ignores Ryn's command. A snarl sounds off behind me, and that finally sends Loa scrambling out of the room.

Zeph shoves me against the cool stone wall of my room and gets in my face. I don't know why I feel so fucking volatile, but I do. Rage, challenge, need, the drive to protect pounds through me, and I feel like I'm drowning in it. I try to bite Zeph, but he just chuckles and presses me into the wall even harder.

"Naughty little sparrow, you know you don't want to hurt me," he coos at me, and he nudges his knee between my legs. Suddenly, that's all I can focus on, and I spread my thighs to make room for more of him. I breathe him in deeply, and Pigeon and I both start to settle.

"Good girl," he praises, and that has me growling at him again.

"You've got the touch," Ryn snarks as he leans against the wall next to me.

Zeph glares at him. Pigeon settles inside of me, and my vision and hands go back to normal. I use my wings to push away from the wall and challenge Zeph's hold. He looks surprised for a moment, but he lets go and scrambles back away from me. "What is going on?" I demand, my head pounding and my stomach groaning for food. "What happened out there?"

Zeph and Ryn shoot a glance at each other, and something about it irritates the fuck out of me. I take a threatening step toward them, ready to lose it. *What the hell is wrong with me?*

"You were having a reaction to the rope that you touched when you freed me," Zeph tells me. "It was Trammel magicked, which keeps whoever is bound by it from shifting. When you broke the magic by cutting it, it must have done something to you," he adds, and Pigeon comes rearing up inside of me.

I blink, and her eyes snap into place. She stares at Zeph and then Ryn, looking for something, but I don't understand what. Ryn looks away, and eventually Zeph does too. Despair fills Pigeon, and she slinks back and releases her hold. I gasp at the devastation that fills me and rub at my chest.

"What just happened?" I demand, but I get nothing from her.

"What did you just do?" I accuse, and my eyes prick with unexplainable tears.

Ryn steps toward me, and I step back away from him, confused. He looks pained, and it's clear there's something going on here that I'm not understanding. Ryn turns to Zeph, his mouth open like he's about to say something, but the look on Zeph's face has Ryn shutting his mouth.

"I told you, after the assignment is complete, we'll figure everything out," Zeph tells Ryn cryptically.

"What aren't you telling me?" I ask quietly, pulling my wings back inside of me with ease as I try and fail to figure out what is happening.

"You've been asleep for a week, Falon. You're hungry and weak, and you should rest and recover. You shouldn't experience any more discomfort now that the toxin has been cleared of your system. You should feel like yourself soon," Zeph reassures me, and then he heads for the door.

Ryn stares at me a beat longer, something I can't identify in his eyes, before he follows Zeph out of the room. His shoulders sag as he leaves me in his wake, and I feel a tug in my gut that wants me to follow him, before I shut it down.

"They're assholes, Pigeon, but so are you for leaving me in the dark. I know that you know what's going on, and I hope this teaches you that they're not for us."

I feel like shit, and I have no idea why. My gryphon is silently lamenting something which makes no sense since Ryn and Zeph are treating me just as indifferently as they always have. I know she likes them—fuck, even I was itching to get Zeph between my thighs—but it is what it is. Hopefully, Pigeon will get over her first failed crush and move on.

Through my whole bath, I try to reassure her and myself that everything will be okay. I focus on Zeph's promise that he would get me home, and I work through everything I need to do as soon as I get back to my world. I hope my bike isn't under a couple feet of snow by now. I get caught up in my worry about the space time continuum, as I get dressed and brush out my wet hair. What if I go back and like fifty years have passed? I was counting on selling my gran's house and using it to open up my own shop. Fuck knows my old job at Roy's isn't going to be waiting for me after I've been gone for at least a couple of months, or worse, maybe longer.

"Falon!" Moro shouts at me from down the hall as I make my way to the kitchens.

"Hey, Moro! How's Tysa?" I ask as he hugs me, and Tysa's tree of a man pats me hard on the back.

"She'll be better now that you're up and moving around. You gave us quite the worry. She's been checking in on you when Loa doesn't chase her away," he tells me, and I warm at his kindness. "She made you a few extra shirts she thinks will work better for you while you're training."

I warm all over at his words. I almost forgot what it was like to talk to people who actually want you around.

"I'm just headed down to fuel up, but when I'm done, I'll come by the house. I think another day's worth of work and everything should be up and running. Then I'll have officially earned all your mate's hard work on my clothes."

"I think you'll have earned a lifetime supply of clothing if you can get warm water out in the surrounding houses and not just here in the stronghold," he admits on a laugh. "I'll let Tysa know; she'll be very excited to see you!" He hugs me again and then proceeds happily down the hall.

I watch him with a smile before my growling stomach reminds me of where I'm supposed to be headed. A child-like giggle pulls my attention away, and I look to find a toddler-sized kid bumbling down the hall to my left. I chuckle and wait for whoever is minding it to come chasing after the child, but no one is in sight. I look around just to double-check, but it's just me and my angry stomach standing here in the hallway.

I frown and turn down the hall after the wobbly little kid. I'm met by echoes of the kid's laughter and glee, but I don't see it in the hall anymore. I hesitate for a second. I don't really like kids all that much, mostly because I have no idea what to do with them. I'm a think-they're-adorable-from-afar kind of girl, but clearly no one is watching this kid, and with open balconies all over the place in this cliff castle, I'd hate for it to have an accident I could have done something to stop.

I follow after the squeals and toddler giggles, picking up my pace as I round a corner, expecting to find the little tyke, but it's once again empty. After a few minutes of repeating my *gotchya* just to have the winding hallway be empty, I start running to catch up. I'm almost at a full blown sprint when I spot the kid at the bottom of some dark stairs.

What the fuck? How the hell did it get down there?

I make my way cautiously down the long flight of stairs that, very ominously, dip down into dimly lit darkness. I'm no longer trusting that anything about this situation is what it seems, but I find myself—probably stupidly—curious about what the hell is going on. Just as I step off the last stair to reach the bottom, the dark hallway lights up with an eerie green light. I clear my throat and white knuckle grip my courage.

"Um... I know there's not really a kid down here, so whoever you are and whatever you want..." I trail off, not sure what the fuck I'm even saying.

A figure, backlit by the green light in the hallway, steps out of nowhere and smiles at me. "Welcome, Daughter of the Shadows. We have been waiting for you," she tells me, her tone ethereal and her movements graceful as she turns around and motions for me to follow her.

"Right, because that's not creepy as fuck," I mumble and then look around, not sure what to do.

If I were in a sketchy movie right now, everyone in the audience would be screaming at me not to follow the creepy glowing chick. I take a step back, intent on fleeing up the stairs and away from The Ghost of Christmas No Fucking Thank You, but I slam up against a wall behind me. I turn around, panicked, and run my hands over the cool stone that now exists where there was just a flight of stairs. *You took your eyes off of her! She's probably right behind you with a fucking axe now!* I whirl around, listening to my inner terrified voice, but to my relief the ghost is still floating down the hallway.

I take another minute to feel around the wall behind me for some latch that might trip the trick door, but all I find is the same smooth, cream-colored stone that the rest of the cliff castle is made out of. *Well, shit.* I scan the rest of the hallway, but there's no other way out. I take a reluctant step forward and then another, internally screaming about how I'm not ready to die.

"You are safe here, child, do not fear. We have been waiting for you," the glowing woman repeats, and I balk, worried she can read my mind.

Where's a tin foil hat when you need one?

"Where exactly is *here*?" I ask as I follow her down what feels like a never-ending hallway.

She doesn't say anything, just continues to do her floaty walk thing until an archway lights up out of nowhere to our left. I gasp as lime green light shines out of symbols and pictures that have been carved into the tall arched stone doors. I suddenly feel sad as I run my eyes over what I think is writing, and I'm driven by the need to reach out and run my hands over every symbol, like I need them to feel me, to know that I'm here. I furrow my brow, puzzled by this odd onslaught of emotion. I check in on Pigeon, but she's asleep at my center, and the feelings don't seem to be radiating out from her.

The green glowing figure moves in front of the doors and leans forward and places a kiss in their middle. She whispers something against the seam of the doors, but I can't make out much of what she was saying. What I can understand strikes a chord of familiarity in me, and I try to place exactly where I've heard it before. A deep boom vibrates around me, making me jump. I crouch, suddenly sure that the walls and ceiling are going to come down on my head at any second. Instead, the old stone doors rumble open slowly, and I stare open-mouthed at what they reveal.

I follow the ghost through the now open archway and look around to find a stone city that's overgrown with vegetation. Moss and climbing greenery are slowly swallowing the cream stone up, but it's massive and stretches as far as I can see. I take another step forward in awe of everything I'm surrounded by.

The green ghostly figure now looks more corporeal. Her smile lights up her whole face, and I gasp, overcome by her beauty. "Welcome, Daughter of the Shadows, to Vedan, the lost city of The Dark Ouphe."

15

Her words bounce around my brain as they try to sink in, and all I can think is *do Zeph and Ryn know this is here*? I look around and stare at the inside of the cliffs. Houses are carved into the walls, and tall buildings rise up and look like they're trying to compete with the massive trees. Light pours in from the open top of the mountain, and I spot other massive sealed doors around me that look exactly like the one I just walked through.

"My name is Nadi, and I was once part of the Ouphe council. My essence was left here to help guide a worthy Bond Breaker such as yourself so that our people can rise from the shadows and once again take their place in this world."

Nadi tells me all of that and then gestures out to the dead city like she's the Vanna White of the Ouphe world. I stare at her warily.

"And exactly how am I supposed to do that?" I ask, not at all liking the sound of *Bond Breaker* and the underlying *you're our only hope*. I'm also not sure that the Ouphe deserve a place in the world if what the Hidden say about them is true.

"You must speak it into existence, and the binding will be undone," she tells me, her face and tone serene.

"And what does that mean? What happens when the binding is undone?"

"Then the Gryphons will be free, and the Ouphe and their magic will no longer be a threat. If the Ouphe people are free from being hunted, then we can once again thrive and rebuild and take our place as the Sentinels of the realm as it should always be," Nadi explains.

"And what keeps you from enslaving the Gryphon like you did before?" I press, not trusting the kumbaya, *everyone will be happy and love each other* part of her plan.

Her silver eyes grow sad, and she motions for me to walk with her toward an overgrown gazebo. I fall into step at her side, watching her white robes sway as she walks. "Our error in judgement has left us on the brink of extinction. We have learned our lesson and have vowed to never repeat the mistakes of our ancestors."

We make our way slowly up the steps of the gazebo, the moss-covered stairs cushioning my steps. I run my hand over a tall clump of heather flowers growing next to the entrance, and the contact fortifies me in a strange way. "Then why haven't you broken the oath and the magic binding the Gryphons to you before?"

"Others have tried," she tells me, her voice pained, and she sits gracefully on a grass-covered bench. "The branch of magic with the ability to break the vow, once and for all, has all but been destroyed. The last full blooded wielder of Bonding Magic was killed twenty sun cycles ago."

She looks at me poignantly, and the hair on my arms stands on end. My father's face rises up in my memories, his green twinkling eyes suddenly reminding me of the green glow of the symbols on the door.

"Your mother's mixed blood held the key, too," Nadi informs me, and I look away from her hopeful eyes.

"How do you know that? How do you know I can even do what you're saying?" I challenge, skepticism pooling inside of me. This all feels a little too convenient for my liking.

"Because, Daughter of the Shadows, you were able to wake me. Only Bond-laced blood can pull my essence to them, can wake up the Ouphe magic woven in the stones of this mountain and every other Ouphe stronghold that has ever been built. Your people know that you are here, that the Bond Breaker once again walks among them. Help them, daughter. They have been waiting so long for you."

I glare at Nadi. "No pressure, right?" I snark and then step back away from her. "I appreciate that your *essence* has been waiting for me," I tell her, raising my hands and putting air quotes around the word essence. "But this is all a little too Lord of the Rings, if you catch my drift. You'll have to forgive me for not just taking your word for it, but given everything that's happened, I think it's best to approach all of this with a serious dose of caution."

Nadi nods and rises from her grass-cushioned seat. "Whatever you feel is right, child. Support will be here for you when you are ready."

And with that, I'm picked up on a breeze and unceremoniously thrown out of the city, the large stone doors slamming shut behind me. I crash into the wall opposite of the arched double doors and crumble to the ground. I glare at the stone entrance, my cheek pressed against the cold stone of the floor.

Well, fuck you too.

I'm painfully aware that I've spent far too much of my life since coming to the Eyrie lying on the floor, tired and pissed off about something. I'm over it. I trace the symbols on the door with my eyes, riding their angles and swirls with my gaze. I get lost in the way that some of them flow into each other, while others stop abruptly and sit solitary and disconnected. I'm not sure how long I lie there staring at the stone doors, but suddenly my name trickles toward me through the dark. I spot a floating orange light in the distance, and I glare at it.

"If you think I'm going to help you with shit after you just threw me out, then your *essence* isn't as wise as you think it is," I tell Nadi and push up from the ground.

My muscles are stiff, and the coolness of the dark hallway nips at my skin. Fuck. How long have I been down here?

"Falon?" a deep voice questions, and then it and the light rush toward me. "Falon, what are you doing down here?" Ryn asks as he bends down and runs his concerned gaze over me.

"You have a dead Ouphe city inside your mountain," I tell him, gesturing to the stone doors as I sit up.

"Yeah, we know. The Ouphe abandoned this place a couple hundred years ago," he tells me, and then he helps me to my feet.

"Apparently, they want to move back in."

"What are you doing down here?" Ryn asks me again. He reaches up and pushes strands of hair out of my face, and I have to stop myself from leaning into his palm.

"Some kid, who wasn't a kid, tricked me down here, and then Nadi showed up with all this *you are our last hope* bullshit, but then she threw me out when I said I'd think about it. Also, I'm pretty sure I heard the walls singing at one point; has that happened to you?"

Ryn stares at me as I ramble, his smoky gray eyes bouncing back and forth between mine, his look becoming more and more worried. My stomach takes that moment to growl its dissatisfaction over everything that's happened. I clamp my hands over it.

"Falon, you should be resting. Have you even eaten anything since you woke up?"

"I was going to, but then..." I point at the door, and Ryn narrows his eyes at me.

"Come on, let's get you back to bed."

I open my mouth to argue that I've been in bed for a week and that I'm not tired, but I realize that's not the case at all. I suddenly feel like the opposite is true and that I haven't slept in a week. Ryn guides me down the short hallway and up the flight of stairs. I keep checking my surroundings, disoriented because this looked different when I was making my way down here.

"Corse," Ryn calls to a guard as we make our way to the hallway where I first spotted the giggling ghost toddler. "Grab a few plates from the kitchen and have them brought up to Z—I mean, Falon's room."

The guard nods and marches off in the direction of the kitchens while we head the opposite way.

"Please," I chastise Ryn.

"What's that?"

"You could say *please*. You know, ask nicely for something. Use manners."

"What do you mean?" Ryn queries, and I scoff.

"Of course you don't know what I mean," I grumble and wave the point of my conversation away.

"No, really, I do want to know what you mean," Ryn presses, and we're back at my room in no time.

"Do gryphons not have words that express gratitude when you ask someone to do something and they do it?" I ask, turning to see Ryn's face.

"We just nod," he answers with a shrug, and I laugh.

"So you never need to soften the blow of being bossy with a *please* or a *thank you*?"

"No, I am second in charge, and what I say or ask for doesn't need to be softened; it just is," he replies. "Where you come from you have to be soft?"

"Sometimes yeah, but I think it's more of an acknowledgement that someone else doesn't *have* to listen to you, but you're grateful that they do. Does that make sense?"

"No," Ryn answers immediately and ushers me toward the bed.

"So I would say, 'Hand me that skin of water, please,' and it would mean you don't have to hand me that skin of water, but I'd be grateful if you do."

"Or you could just say, 'Hand me that skin of water,' and know that the person you asked will do it and that's that," Ryn argues.

"Well, that's easy for you to say though, because you have power as the *second in charge*," I mock. "So people *have* to listen to you. But what if you didn't have that authority?"

"Then you'd get the skin of water for yourself." He looks at me, his gray gaze puzzled, and I can't help but smile.

"Okay fine, manners aren't for gryphons, I concede the point," I offer with my hands up in surrender.

"Giving up so easily, Falon? And here I was thinking you were a fighter," he teases, and I laugh.

"Oh don't you worry, Altern, I'll get a please out of you before I leave, just you wait and see."

Ryn's eyebrows drop, and his gaze grows troubled. "What do you mean *before you leave*?"

I run my eyes over his face, unsure of the emotion I'm seeing there. Worry? No that doesn't seem right.

"Zeph promised that when we got back here, he'd take me home. So I'll probably be leaving in a couple days," I explain, and Ryn's features go steely with anger.

"Did he now?" Ryn responds, but it feels more like a condemnation than a question. He backs away from me and stomps toward the door.

"Where are you going?" I demand.

"To speak with Zeph."

"Oh no you don't!" I command and scramble to put myself in his way. "I want to go home. It's time. I'm grateful for what I learned about myself and Pigeon, but I don't belong here."

"I don't have time to discuss this with you, but you will stay here until I'm back." Ryn slashes his hand out in a gesture that clearly communicates that he thinks his word is final.

"The fuck I will," I growl at him and move forward to crowd his space even more. "Where are you going?" I ask suddenly and then shake my head to clear it of curiosity. "It doesn't matter. I'm going home, and there isn't shit you can do about that."

Ryn stalks forward until my back is pressed against the door. Pigeon sits up inside of me, and I have to fight not to roll my eyes at her. "I have an assignment. I'll be back in a couple of weeks. And I promise you, Falon, you will be here when I walk back through these doors. Zeph will ensure it. He has just as much at stake in all of this as I do."

"And just what the fuck does that mean?" I demand, pushing at his chest to try and give myself some space. He doesn't budge.

"I don't have time to explain it right now. Just stay here until I get back." His intense stare drops from mine, and he takes a step back.

I'm once again punched in the face with the feeling that I'm missing something here, and I'm fucking over it. "No," I answer, and his steely gaze shoots back up to mine, his irises a now furious bubbling mercury. "I don't know exactly what is going on here, but I'm not a complete fucking idiot. You and Zeph are hiding something that has to do with me, and yet neither one of you have the balls to tell me what's up," I rage at him. "I've been lied to my whole life apparently, which is probably why you two assholes think you can get away with it, but I've officially hit my limit of bullshit. I don't care what is going on, and I *am* leaving. I don't want to be involved in your world or your little war anymore. I have a life to get back to and the mystery of my existence to solve. So you can just fuck o—"

Ryn's lips are suddenly on mine, and he swallows down the rest of my angry rant. He cups my face and tries to pull me closer to him, but I shove him away, breaking the kiss.

"What the fuck, Ryn?" I demand as I try to ignore the heat unfurling inside of me.

His gaze is molten, and the need suddenly radiating off of him calls to my own. He doesn't answer my question with words. He just cups my face again and slams his lips back down to mine. I breathe in his hunger as he coaxes me into a response, kissing my top lip and then my bottom, encouraging me to open for him.

His lips feel so fucking good against my own, and with Pigeon flashing me encouraging images of gryphon porn, I relent and open up to Ryn. I snake my tongue out to tease his, and he growls into my mouth. The kiss deepens and starts to morph into something else entirely. It feels more like a claiming than a lust-filled exchange, but he's so fucking good at it, I don't even care.

His tongue teases and swirls with mine, and I pass all control over into his expert hands. He cups my head, his thumbs resting on my cheek bones and guiding my head in whatever direction that allows him to claim my mouth how he wants. I moan as he presses me into the wall next to the door, and then he reaches down, never breaking our kiss, and lifts me up so he can grind into me. I wrap my legs around his thick torso and roll my hips against the erection begging to be freed from his pants.

Ryn grabs my ass and encourages me to do that again, and we both moan at the delicious friction when I do. Need fills our kiss, and I tug at his shirt and grind down on him, wanting more. I pull his shirt up and off, forcing our lips apart, and he does the same with my top. I reach down to untie his pants, but the perplexed look on his face makes me pause.

"What's wrong?" I ask breathlessly.

"What is that?" he demands and gestures to my chest.

"It's a bra." I chuckle.

"Make it...go away," he commands, and I can't help but laugh.

If I weren't so fucking horny, I might make him figure it out on his own, but I am, so I reach down and untie the laces in the front that keep the binding in place. Ryn watches hungrily, transfixed by what I'm doing, and as soon as the laces are free, he pushes my bra off my shoulders and bends down and sucks hard on a needy nipple.

"Fuck yes," I encourage and run my fingers through his light brown hair and hold his head right where it's at.

He flicks at my nipple with his tongue, and it shoots sensations straight to my clit. I moan as he continues to do it while simultaneously reaching around and squeezing my ass hard. Now this is the kind of manhandling a girl can get down with. He sucks hard on my boob and then pops off and turns his attention to my other rock hard nipple. He growls as I tug at his hair to pull him away, but I'd rather he sucked on me while he was fucking me, and I'd prefer that he start fucking me right now.

The door to the room flies open. "Corse said you requested food. I thought I'd bring it up and check on..."

Zeph freezes as soon as he spots us, and I watch his features morph from concerned to furious. "What in rutting fairies do you think you're doing?" he bellows at Ryn, who takes a step away from me to get in Zeph's face.

Zeph drops the tray of food to answer Ryn's challenge, and the smell of meat and bread waft up from the floor to remind me that I'm still starving.

"You told her you were going to take her back home?" Ryn demands, his fists balling up as he squares off with Zeph.

Zeph looks past Ryn to me for a second and then refocuses on his second in command. "I did," he answers tersely.

"So, what? You send me away and take her back when I'm gone? Was that the plan? Is this urgent assignment even legitimate? Or do you just need to get me out of the way so you can rid yourself of her and the connection?" Ryn accuses, and I don't miss the flash of hurt in Zeph's eyes before he masks it with anger. He doesn't answer Ryn's question, and Ryn rounds on me.

"Tell me you'll stay until I come back." He steps into me and cups my face. He has desperation in his eyes, and I have no fucking clue why. "Tell me, Falon, vow to me that you will stay here until I get back."

Ryn gives me a little shake, pulling me from my scattered thoughts, and Zeph growls in warning behind him. My eyes snap to Zeph, who looks like he wants to rip someone's head off. I don't know if it's his anger or Ryn's desperation that spurs me on, but I look back to Ryn, my gaze searching. I can practically see the please in his eyes even though he doesn't voice it.

"Okay," I tell him, and as the word leaves my lips, Ryn bends down to taste it.

He kisses me just enough to leave me panting. He pulls away, and my hungry gaze traces his every muscle as he bends over and snatches his shirt from the ground and storms past Zeph, bumping his shoulder aggressively as he leaves. I wait for Zeph to respond, but he just watches me, his chest heaving and weighed down with anger. I stand there shirtless, pissed that he interrupted and irritated that I just agreed to be here for who knows how much longer.

Zeph takes a step toward me and then stops himself. He seems to be warring about something internally, and I just stand there and try to decipher the emotions flitting through his features. Heat, anger, confusion, and resolve flash across his face so quickly I almost can't track it. A plate crunches beneath his boot as he takes another step, and the sound snaps Zeph out of whatever trance he's in.

"Get your own food," he snarls at me and then stomps out of the room, slamming the door behind him.

The closing door hits a plate and sends it sliding into the wall. A turquoise piece of duda fruit bounces off the sliding plate and stops just shy of my foot. I stare at the door for a beat, not sure what the fuck just happened. *Well, it looks like another night of self-entertainment is in the cards for me,* I grumble to myself and kick the turquoise piece of fruit away from me. Fucking confusing and volatile gryphons. I run my fingers through my hair and let out an exasperated sigh.

What's a girl gotta do around here to get some ass?

16

"Wait. He just walked in? What did you do?" Tysa asks, her eyes wide with shock, and her hands covering her mouth.

"I just stood there. What was I going to do? They had a pissing match about something, and Ryn just left. Here, hand me that bolt."

Tysa looks around until she identifies what I'm pointing at and hands it to me. "Oh come on, Falon, not even you can be that unobservant. They had a pissing match, but you have no idea what about?" She rolls her eyes at me.

"If you're insinuating it was about me, then you're way off the mark. They can barely even look at me without the contempt dripping from their eyes. Just look at Zeph if you don't believe me. He's been avoiding me at all costs the past couple weeks. That is not the actions of someone who is interested."

Tysa snorts, and I stop what I'm doing and glare at her.

"Oh, Moro hit on you that way?" I challenge. "He sniffed your neck, promised to take you back where you came from, and then avoided you like the plague?"

She smiles and fingers a lock of her almond-colored

hair. "No, he made it clear he wanted to claim me right away."

"See, exactly. I'm not even trying to lock anyone down; I'm just trying to scratch an itch. I thought Zeph or Ryn would be excellent back scratchers, but in the end, they just leave me itchier and then act like I have some kind of disease."

"Who has a disease?" Moro asks as he walks out of the back of the house to where we are.

He kisses Tysa sweetly, and when they pull apart, they share a look of such complete devotion, I have to look away. I rub at my chest and the ache I suddenly feel there.

"No one has a disease. Falon's just having some trouble getting her rut on," Tysa tells her mate, and I chuck a dirty rag at her.

Moro catches it and keeps it from hitting his mate, and I give him an exasperated look. I tighten the last of the bolts on the tank I've spent the past couple weeks constructing. And clap my hands once.

"Alright, I think that should do it. Go see if it works," I announce, and Tysa starts hopping around excitedly before rushing toward her house.

I cross my fingers and give Moro a *here goes nothing* look. He smiles at me, and then we wait. Tysa screams, and a beaming smile creeps over my face. She comes running out of the back of the house and right into her mate's arms. He laughs and swings her around a couple times before setting her down. I let out an *oomph* as Tysa catches me in a solid tackle hug, and we both start laughing as we crash to the ground.

"You did it! I can't believe you actually did it!" Tysa squeals. "Moro, we have hot water just like they do in the stronghold!"

"I told you I could do it, but it's good to know you didn't believe me," I tease, and Tysa wraps me up in another hug.

When she told me the trade that she wanted from me for the clothes, I wasn't sure how hard it would be to pull off. But Tysa introduced me to their metalsmith, Mison, and he said he would make all the tools and things I needed if I agreed to get hot water to his house too.

"The rest of the row is going to be so envious, I'm telling you, Falon. When they hear that you pulled it off, they'll all be looking to trade for you to do the same thing for their houses," Tysa tells me, and I shrug.

I start packing up the few tools I was able to explain to Mison well enough for him to make, and give the tank and pipes one last look to make sure nothing is leaking or has come loose.

"You are coming tonight, aren't you?" Tysa asks me as I finish up my inspection.

"I wasn't planning on it." The last thing I want to do is to go to some stuffy event with a bunch of people who can barely stand the sight of me.

"Oh come on, Falon, it will be fun! The seasons only change three times a year, and this celebration is the best. Everyone drinks and dances all night in thanks to the warmth and all it gave us, and to welcome the cold. Which will be so much easier to manage now that we have hot water!" She squeals with excitement again, and I can't help but laugh. "I still have that other dress I made you that you haven't worn. It would be perfect for tonight."

"Could help you with that rutting problem you say you're having," Moro announces playfully, and I shoot him a glare.

"Fine," I grumble and then yelp as Tysa starts pulling me toward the house.

"I have an iron I've been dying to try out on your hair,"

she announces, and I look back at her mate, my eyes begging for help. Moro hold his hands up in surrender and chuckles, his loving eyes alight with happiness for his mate and her excitement.

* * *

"Tysa, I can't wear this!" I insist as I take in the deep teal, satin-like fabric that barely covers any part of my body.

"Why? You look gorgeous!" she argues, confused by my incredulity.

"I'm practically naked," I point out, and she just rolls her eyes.

"It will be hot tonight. There will be fires and dancing. You will thank me later. Other women will be wearing similar styles; just look at my dress."

I look over to where she has her clothes laid out on a chair. She has a long silver skirt and a band of fabric that looks like it's the top. I release a sigh and then return my stare to the mirror Tysa just parked me in front of. The dress has spaghetti straps that hold up the triangles of teal fabric that cover my boobs but display a lot of cleavage. There's about four inches of smooth satiny fabric that fits tight to my waist, and from there, it's basically a long panel of fabric covering my crotch and another long panel of fabric covering my ass.

Aside from my hard nipples being very obvious, if I don't move, the dress doesn't look that risqué. The issue is, as soon as I do move, the high slits that go up to the bottom of my ribs on both of my sides are very obvious, and if the wind decides to get frisky, it won't take much to be flashing pussy and ass to everyone.

"I just don't want the whole awkward overdressed thing

that happened when the alarms went off to happen again," I tell Tysa, and she gives my arm a squeeze before combing through my now straight white hair.

"Trust me, tonight, all the women get dressed up and celebrate, you'll see. And I will say, if ever there was a dress that would solve a rutting problem, this would be the dress."

I laugh and take one last look in the mirror. The color is gorgeous, and as worried as I am about standing out in a bad way, I do feel sexy as fuck. I brush my thick white hair back over my shoulder, and it almost hits my lower back. I take a deep fortifying breath, turn away from the mirror, and give Tysa a nod.

"Okay, let's do this," I concede.

Tysa squees and then proceeds to get dressed in her two piece flowy silver number. She takes the band of fabric and wraps it around the back of her neck, crosses it at her chest to cover her boobs, and ties it off behind her back. Her skirt only has one slit up the side, but I instantly feel better seeing that she's showing a lot of skin too.

Moro takes in his mate as we step out of the room. His gaze grows heated, and I get the distinct impression that if I weren't here, he'd move that slit in her dress over and fuck the shit out of his mate. Tysa blushes from his approving gaze, and I once again rub at my chest in an effort to banish the ache.

"Shall we?" Moro asks and extends his arm out to Tysa. She takes it, and he leans down and whispers something in her ear that has Tysa giggling and nuzzling into his side.

I follow them out the door, and goose bumps rise up all over my body from the cool breeze that brushes past me. I put my hands down to make sure my crotch and ass flap of fabric don't go crazy and start flashing my bits. We join a group of other people who are all making their way out into the forest for the celebration. Their jovial conversation washes over me, and I stare up at the stars that are just starting to wake up in the sky and twinkle their hello. Gentle wind plays with the leaves in the trees, and shadows stretch out in our path like they're trying to join us for the party too.

Our group crests a hill, and I see three large bonfires that are spread throughout the clearing. There are long tables spilling over with food, and casks filled with different drinks speckled all around. Some people are already dancing. They're gathered in a group between the large pyres, weaving in and out of each other as they play tag with their smiles and laughter. There's a lightness to everyone that I haven't experienced yet while living among them, and it feels contagious.

Moro leads Tysa to the food, and I follow in true awkward third wheel fashion. I pile up a plate and stuff my face while I watch the flames try to keep time with the music and the dancers.

"Falon?"

I look up at the sound of my name to find Sutton staring at me wide-eyed.

"I thought that was you," he admits as he closes the distance.

I try to swallow down the massive bite of meat and flat-bread that I just shoved in my mouth and give him a smile.

"You look...stunning," Sutton tells me, his mouth wrapping around the word *stunning* in a very appealing way. He takes me in, and I like the way his eyes dip and caress over my curves and exposed skin.

"You clean up well," I respond in turn, and I smile even wider at the blush that sneaks into his cheeks.

I'm used to seeing him in armor, sweaty and dirty from training, with his hair pulled back. But tonight, his golden-streaked brown hair falls in waves around his shoulders. He's tan and clean and looks good enough to eat.

"Who do I have to thank for this dress?" Sutton teases, and I laugh.

"Tysa." At the sound of her name, Tysa looks over, and Sutton gestures to me and then gives her a deep bow. Tysa laughs and then wags her eyebrows at me before Sutton straightens up and catches it. I give Tysa a wink, and she grabs Moro's arm and drags him out to join the dancers.

"How's it coming along with Ami?" Sutton asks as he moves to stand next to me, his big well-muscled arm brushing against me.

"Good. We're making progress," I offer vaguely and watch as Moro twirls a giggling Tysa around.

"Do you feel like you and your gryphon are connecting, becoming one?"

I shrug noncommittally, not sure what to say. I have been making progress with Ami. As soon as he replaced all the items that were destroyed with his little cliff stunt, I put everything behind me, and we got to work on shifting. Pigeon and I are finding a good balance, but I don't think we'll ever be the kind of *one* that Sutton is with his gryphon. Ami was right in saying that Pigeon and I might always feel like two separate entities sharing the same body. I, of course, don't tell Sutton any of this, because I don't want him to look at me the way the others do as they spit *highborn* or *blood tainted* at me whenever it suits them.

Sutton doesn't press for details, and we fall into a companionable silence as we watch the dancers bouncing and laughing.

"Would you like to dance?" Sutton asks me, and my eyes snap up to his.

"Um...I don't know how. I mean, I know how to dance, but I don't know the moves to the dances you do," I correct.

"I'd be happy to teach you," Sutton offers, and I don't miss the way his tone lowers, a hint of suggestion in it.

"I don't think this dress could handle one of the twirly dances without flashing lips and crack to everyone, but maybe the next little bouncy one would be safe," I hedge, and Sutton's smile becomes beaming.

"A drink then? To fortify our courage for the next bouncy one," he offers, and with my nod, he quickly tromps off into the direction of the closest cask.

I smile as I watch him weave through people, and make a mental note to high five Tysa tomorrow after I've spent all night scratching all of my itches with Sutton. I feel eyes on me, and I slowly scan the faces around me, looking for whoever is setting my senses off. I land on an intense honey-filled gaze, and I'm not sure how I feel about Zeph staring at me so intently. I haven't seen him for weeks, and I hate that something wakes up inside of me as I return his stare, refusing to be the one to look away first.

A creamy delicate hand reaches up to caress Zeph's cheek, and it's then that I notice the woman sitting in his lap. Her dress looks like the first dress Tysa made for me, and I don't miss that Zeph's hand is tucked into the front drape of fabric. She rubs the scruff on his square jaw and whispers something into his ear. I feel furious and betrayed and find myself rubbing at the ache in my chest. Pigeon wants to fly over there and shred this bitch into a million pieces, but I hold her back. She needs to see the truth once and for all so she can let this fucked up crush go.

Zeph breaks eye contact when the girl in his lap pulls his lips down to hers, and I look away, not sure if I want to rage, run, or fuck that image out of my head. Sutton returns right then and hands me a large stein full of something. I take it from him and immediately start chugging it down.

"Mmm, what is this?" I ask as I take a break from swallowing down half the stein's contents.

Sutton laughs and then reaches up and wipes away a

foam mustache from my top lip with his thumb. He pops his thumb in his mouth, and it's hot as fuck. "It's meade," he tells me and then takes a deep pull of his own mug, his sage green eyes alight with heat.

"Fuck it, let's dance," I order as I slam back the rest of my meade and drop the empty cup on the closest table. Sutton does the same, laughing as I grab his hand and pull him out amidst the other dancers.

"I thought the twirly ones were bad," he tells me on a laugh, stepping closer to me so I can hear him over the music and other couples.

I lean into him, wrapping my hand around the back of his neck and pulling his ear close to my lips. "Well, you look like the big, strong, protective type. Think you can protect my virtue while we're out on this dance floor?" I tease. I pull back, and Sutton's pupils dilate as his eyes lock on to my lips.

"Now, show me your moves, big guy!"

17

I fan my face as Sutton takes my hand and drags me off the dance floor. I'm flushed from laughter and movement, and smiling from ear to ear.

"I'll grab us a drink," he shouts over the noise, and I nod and point to where I'll wait for him.

I weave my way over to our meeting point and release a relieved breath as the cloying heat of the fires dissipates, and I'm greeted by cooler air on the outskirts of the partying crowd. I spot the top of the cliff castle between the trees, and I give it my back as I turn and scan the crowd for Sutton. I spot him, two steins in hand, and wave him over.

"You're an excellent dancer," I offer as I accept the stein he hands my way and take a huge gulp. The sweet cold drink tastes amazing, and I moan at the flavor that explodes all over my tongue.

"Me? I was just trying to keep up with you. I thought you said you didn't know these dances," he tells me as he gulps his whole mug down in three seconds.

"I don't, but they weren't hard to pick up at all. They remind me of this dance I once saw in *A Knight's Tale.*"

"Who has a tail?" Sutton asks confused.

I laugh and wave the question away. "There were a lot more steps, but it reminds me of a more lyrical version of line dancing, which is a dance that people do where I come from. Although, I think the way my people dance most of the time would probably traumatize the entire Eyrie," I admit, and I chuckle at the thought of the look on everyone's face if I went out on the dance floor and twerked.

"How so?" Sutton asks, his eyes lit up with amusement.

The moon's light plays with the golden highlights in his long hair, and I find myself momentarily distracted. "What?"

"Why would the Eyrie be traumatized by the way your people dance?" he clarifies.

"Oh right. Because typically, if you were to go to a club or something, you'd find a lot of people grinding on each other." Suttons confused look makes me smile. "That's a dance where the couple writhes and rubs up on each other like they're having sex, but they're not actually having sex," I explain, and I track Sutton's tongue as it darts out and wets his lips.

"Even our slow dances are way more intimate," I tell him as I take his drink out of his hands.

I set both of our mugs on the ground and then step into Sutton. I grab his large hands and place them on my hips, and then I reach up and wrap my hands around his neck. I have to stand on my tiptoes, and Sutton bends down a little to make it easier for me, which makes me laugh.

"Fuck, you're tall," I observe as I pull his body flush with mine. I feel his breath hitch, and I like knowing I have this effect on him.

"You're beautiful," he answers back, and he groans a little when I play with the hair on the back of his head. "So once you get in position, then what?" he asks, tightening his hold on my hips.

Heat fills me, and I run my gaze from his eyes to his lips.

"Then you just sway," I explain, showing him how to move his weight from one foot to the other. "You spin in a little circle, swaying like this, and just feel each other."

"I think I like the way your people dance much better than the way mine do," he admits, and I laugh.

Sutton leans down to close the distance between our lips. I smile in encouragement and close my eyes.

Finally!

His full pout barely skims mine before he pulls away suddenly. I open my eyes, a sound of protest sitting on my tongue, but I blanch when I see Zeph shoving Sutton away from me.

Are you fucking kidding me?

Sutton looks confused by Zeph's actions. He's pushing back as if to defend himself from his leader but not escalating things beyond that.

Zeph bellows, "Mine," in Sutton's face, and his sage gaze widens with surprise.

"I didn't know, Syta, I would never..." Sutton defends, and then he throws up his hands in surrender. He shoots me a disappointed look and then turns and walks away.

What the fuck?

"Sutton!" I shout out and try to go after him, but Zeph steps in my way.

Pigeon wakes up inside of me, and my vision changes as I get ready to shift and let her deal with this asshole.

Zeph grabs my neck and leans down into my face. "Mine, little sparrow!" he growls at me, and I'm completely floored when I feel Pigeon practically melt into a puddle of mush inside of me.

"Pigeon, what in the actual fuck are you doing?" I demand, but she's already backed off, and I know I'm not going to get any help from her in dealing with this prick.

"Sutton!" I shout out again, but he just walks away,

shoulders slumped, leaving me to deal with Zeph all on my own.

My chest aches with the rejection, and I turn my furious gaze on Zeph. "That is the second motherfucking time you've been a raging, cock block, douchebag! What the hell is your problem?" I yell at him, shoving at his chest, more pissed than I have ever felt in my life. I want to kill him.

"You will not look at, let alone entertain, another gryphon again!" he shouts at me, and I see fucking red.

"You will not fucking tell me what I can and can't do, let alone *who* I can and can't do. I am a grown ass woman who likes sex, and I'll fuck whoever I want! And there isn't shit you can say or do about it!" I scream back.

Zeph says nothing, just picks me up and slams me over his shoulder and stomps back toward the castle.

"What the fuck are you doing? Put me down!" I demand, but of course he fucking doesn't.

"Pigeon!" I scream internally. *"You better wake the fuck up, you lazy turkey, because I am not dealing with this shit on my own!"*

"If I have to lock you up, little sparrow, I will, but you will obey me," Zeph snarls, pulling me from my internal battle with my useless gryphon as he carries me inside the cliff castle and starts up the stairs to get to my room.

"Pigeon!" I try again. Nothing.

"You don't fucking own me. Your orders don't mean shit to me. Who the fuck are you to tell me anything?" I demand.

Zeph slams open the door to my room and pulls me off of his shoulder. As soon as I'm on my feet, I immediately move to get into his face.

"I am the leader of these people, and what I say is final!" he bellows at me, his yell sending strands of my hair flying back away from my face.

"You are nothing to me, and what you say doesn't mean

shit!" I snap back.

Zeph charges, and I reach back a closed fist, ready to pummel him as much as I can. He grabs my face and slams his lips to mine. I'm momentarily shocked by what the hell he's doing, but my synapses start firing off again, and I punch him in the side of his head. My hit doesn't even faze him, and he mistakes my mouth opening in shock as an invitation for him to deepen his unwanted kiss. I punch him again and bite his tongue.

He hisses and pulls back. I swing for him again, but he catches my fist and tries to lean down to apply another kiss to my outraged lips.

"What the fuck is your problem?" I shout at him as I struggle to do something that will hurt him and expel my rage.

"You are mine to command, mine to do what I please with, even your animal recognizes the truth of this!" Zeph growls at me.

I pounce on him, kicking, scratching, and biting. I want to draw blood; I want to shred him like Pigeon shredded those hunters in the woods. I need him to hurt. I need him to suffer the way he's made me suffer.

Wait. What?

I pause, confused, as the intense thoughts flit through my mind mid-attack. Zeph pulls me off of him and crushes his full lips against mine again.

"Don't fight, little sparrow, you know you're mine. I'm tired of fighting it, and I know you must be too," Zeph speaks against my mouth. "Feel the truth, little sparrow, you know you can feel the pull, the connection."

He kisses me harder, and his taste confuses me even more. I have so many emotions swirling inside of me right now, and I have no idea what to make of any of it. I moan involuntarily as Zeph strokes my tongue with his and then sucks on my bottom lip. His kiss is bruising, and I hate that I fucking love it. I thread my hands into his long curly black hair and pull it. He growls in response and works harder to own my mouth.

I bite him again and pull back, my furious gaze matching the fire I see in his molten honey stare. "I am no one's. I belong to no one!" I growl in his face, and then I kiss him hard, stealing back my control. I claim his lips and guide his tongue with my own. I drive the kiss the way I want it and grind against him the way that feels good to me, not giving a fuck if he likes it or not.

He grabs my ass and lifts me up on his body and slams my back against a pillar. His "mine" fills my kiss, and he kneads my ass, driving more heat to pulse through my body.

"Not in a million fucking years," I argue back between deep tongue strokes that feel so fucking good and make me so fucking wet that it pisses me off.

I don't want to like what he's doing to me. I want to be pissed and outraged over the audacity and arrogance he's displayed. But his hands feel right on my body, his tongue was made to play with mine. I need to ride his cock and claim his body. And if I have to wait any longer to do any of that, I feel like it will be the end of me.

I know Pigeon is at play here, that she's somehow over-riding logic with some serious fucking hormones, but I'm so wet and so fucking needy, I just don't care. I grab the *V* of Zeph's red shirt, where the laces start, and pull at the fabric. It rips down his front, and he growls into my mouth with approval. He grabs the straps of my top and tugs at them, popping them off with no effort. The triangles of fabric covering my boobs fold down like they're bowing to Zeph and his sexual prowess.

My irritation over that is lost when Zeph pulls his mouth from mine and bends over to suck on my hard, sensitive nipple. I moan and grind against him, but the delicious zings he's sending straight to my clit are suddenly replaced by pain as he bites down too hard on my breast. I slap his head away and try to push him off me.

"Ow, you fucker, what the hell was that for?" I don't miss the twinkle of amusement in his eyes as he ignores my question and tries to suck on me again. I push against him and get just enough room between us to land a knee in his side. Zeph gasps and grabs his stomach. I slide down the pillar, no longer pinned by his massive body, and I wiggle away from him, making a beeline for the door.

Fuck this, asshole!

His massive hand snakes out and clamps around my arm, pulling me back to him. "Where do you think you're going?"

"To find a less annoying cock to fuck!" I snarl at him and try to peel his fingers off my arm.

"You are mine!" His yell fills the room, and we start to wrestle.

I poke his eye, and he lets me go. I make it a step away from him before he trips me and then pounces. I pinch his nipple, and he bites at my neck. I moan and then go still, wondering why the fuck that made me moan. Zeph releases a knowing chuckle which results in me punching him in the throat and making him choke on it. I scramble out from underneath him as he's trying to recover, but he grabs my ass flap of fabric and yanks me back down on top of him. I land, all elbows, and try to get away, but his fist in the last remnants of my dress are making it difficult.

Pigeon is fucking loving this, and I give her the side-eye as I roll on top of Zeph until we're chest to chest, and then I lean down and bite down hard on his nipple. His groan is all gravel and need, and he thrusts his hips up, his pants-clad erection rubbing against my ass.

"I need to be inside of you, now!" Zeph demands, and then he rips off the rest of my dress.

"Take your fucking pants off then," I order, and then I seize possession of his mouth again.

I straddle his chiseled abs and grind down on them, moaning at the friction of my clit on his hard muscles. We mouth fuck as he struggles with the laces of his pants, and we both practically cheer when he finally gets them off. He tries to flip me on my back, but I slam him back down. We both go a little wide-eyed at my sudden strength, and I internally high five Pigeon for her help. It's about time she got on board with the *take what we want* plan.

I reach back between my thighs for Zeph's cock, stroking it once as I line him up with me. I'm practically dripping and in no need of foreplay, but I rub the head of his cock through my folds and revel in the look on Zeph's face as I do. He lifts his hips off the ground in an effort to hurry me, but I avoid letting him take control.

I glare at him, and he growls at me, digging his demanding fingers into my hips. I clench down as I fit the tip of him inside of me, eager to be full of him and on my way to an orgasm. I watch Zeph's face as I slowly lower myself on top of him and smile when he groans and throws his head back as the inside of my thighs press against his hips. Zeph encourages me to move right away, but I take a minute to appreciate how deep he is and how full I feel before rising up and then dropping back down on him.

I set a hurried pace, not interested in anything but a mind-blowing orgasm on Zeph's massive cock. I lean forward, my hands on his chest for leverage, and fuck him until the rage in my chest starts to dissipate and I'm lost to the sensation of riding him. Zeph sits up and captures a nipple in his mouth, sucking hard and moaning. We're both panting, and he squeezes my ass every time I rise up, and lets go when I drop my hips back down so that he spears deep inside of me.

I squeal when Zeph suddenly stands up and steals my fucking reins. He holds me tightly to him so that he's deep inside of me as he moves us to the bed. He's surprisingly gentle as he lays me down on my back and presses into me. He brushes a few white strands of hair from my face and then sears his lips to mine in a desperately hungry and perfectly bruising kiss. I unhook my legs from around his waist and let my thighs fall open, giving him as much room as he needs to fuck me hard.

Our tongues swirl together, as he pinches a nipple between his fingers, and then he starts pounding into me, hard and relentless. I break the kiss so I can shout out my approval, and Zeph growls into my ear and nips at my lobe.

"You. Are. Mine," he snarls into my ear, each word punctuated by a deep punishing thrust.

I moan and gasp and beg for more, harder, faster, and the fucking asshole gives it to me. My whole body lights up with tingles, and I can feel that the impending orgasm is going to be so fucking good. Each hard thrust moves me higher up on the bed until we're both pushing off against the headboard. I use it as leverage to angle my hips just a little bit higher, and it takes everything to a whole new level for me. I clench around Zeph, so close to falling over the best fucking orgasm cliff.

"Come for me, little sparrow," Zeph commands.

My eyes fly open, and I glare at him. "Make me, asshole."

Zeph smiles and eagerly accepts my challenge. He drops his head and sucks on my nipple and then pinches the other one hard. He fucks me hard and fast, and in no time, I'm falling over the edge as an incredible orgasm explodes through my body. I reach between us and rub at my clit, trying to milk this sensation for all it's worth. Zeph watches me for a minute as I writhe underneath him, riding the wave of tingles and heat. He slaps my hand away and pulls out of me, crawling down my body until his mouth is latched onto my clit.

My still orgasming pussy clenches around nothing, but I stop caring as Zeph sucks on me, and I grind up into his mouth. A purring sound fills the room. I sit up trying to figure out what the hell is going on, when an intense vibration presses against my clit. I give a surprised shout and watch Zeph's face between my thighs.

I moan as another orgasm quickly builds and shove my hand in his hair. "Fuck! Right there," I command as Zeph rotates his head, and the vibration hits an even sweeter spot right at the top of my clit. "Oh fuck! How are you doing that? Yes, stay right fucking there! Oh fuck yes!" I scream out as I fall into another orgasm. I roll my hips and try to remove my sensitive bundle of nerves from Zeph's still vibrating mouth, but he pins me down and forces me into a third screaming orgasm.

I'm not normally a screamer, so the fact that I am now is blowing my mind. I barely have time to even process that before Zeph's massive cock is moving in and out of me again, and I'm reduced to a moaning, mewling, incoherent mess. He feels so fucking good, and when he demands that I say I am his, I don't even pause before telling him exactly what he wants to hear.

On the word *yours*, he presses as deeply inside of me as he can get and roars out his release. He nips at my neck as he rides out his orgasm and then rolls us over so that I'm once again on top of him. Neither of us say a word as our panting slows into deep measured breaths. Zeph's quiet snores vibrate through my chest, and I don't even care that he's still inside of me as I close my eyes and quickly fall into the deep darkness of satisfied sleep.

18

An echo of my dad's voice floats around my head. He and my mom are talking, but I can't make out about what. Gentle fingers smooth hair away from my face, and I squeeze tighter around my mother's neck. I'm crying, and they're arguing.

"She didn't mean to, Awlon. You can't get mad at her for doing something she doesn't understand. She's only four."

"I'm not mad at her, Noor, but if any of my kind feel what she just did, they will come looking, and we both know that will not end well for anyone."

My dad's voice is laced with worry. I feel bad even though my mom is trying to soothe it away with gentle touches and cuddles.

"We need to move, and not to another city. If her abilities are manifesting already, then we need to keep to ourselves as much as possible until we can find another cladding stone."

"I'm sorry, daddy, I was just trying to play princess like they do in the movie." I sob into my mother's neck, and my dad pulls me out of her arms and hugs me.

"Shhh, don't cry, my heart. Don't cry. We'll make it okay." My dad pulls back and wipes at my cheeks. I look into his bright green eyes and feel the love and concern spilling out of them.

"Falon, my heart, you have to promise me not to make anything other than yourself obey you again. Do you understand?"

I just stare at him.

"Maybe you should have never taught her the language," Gran snaps at dad.

Mom silences her with a look, and my gran stomps away, mumbling angrily under her breath.

"Tamod is a bad word?" I ask, and my dad's eyes bounce back and forth between mine.

"A word is never bad, but bad things can be done with words, and we must make sure that we keep ourselves and others from doing that."

I nod at him, and he wraps me in a tight hug.

"We will both have to do better," he tells me as he kisses my cheek, and I hug him harder.

Loss sears through me, and I whimper at its icy touch. Sadness burns coldly through my veins, and I thrash uncomfortably. I slowly wake up from sleep. By the time I get my eyes open, the strange feeling has almost receded, and the memory I've never looked back on before is an echo in my chest. I'm tangled in my sheets, sweating my ass off, and feeling achy like I worked out way too hard the day before. I sit up and look around the room. There's no sign of Zeph, other than his dry cum on my thigh. I wrinkle my nose at that realization and untangle myself from the sheets.

I feel better after a long bath. I wash all evidence of last night's exploits from my body and don't feel nearly as sore and ragged when I'm done as I did when I first woke up. I check my body for marks or bruising, but there's nothing there that needs to be hidden. Strangely my skin looks almost glowy, my hair is shinier than I ever remember seeing it, and my lavender-colored eyes look downright radiant. Either the food here has some nutrients that my body has been lacking, or sex seriously does my body good.

As mind-blowing as last night with Zeph was, I don't think it would be good for me or for Pigeon to tap that ass anymore in the future. Besides, if that purring tongue thing is something all gryphons can do, then we can get plenty of good sex elsewhere. My first order of business today is to talk to Sutton and find out what the hell happened last night. I tie the laces to my bra and pull up my pants just as Ami comes flying in through my balcony.

"Knock much?" I chastise as I reach for my shirt.

"Rut much?" he snarks back, sniffing at the room and wagging his eyebrows.

"Touché," I offer as I pull my shirt over my head.

When I pop my head through the neck, I notice that Ami is doing his whole white-eye thing at me.

"Interesting," he observes and then shields his eyes with his hand like he's staring at something bright.

I just stare at him and wait for him to explain what the hell he's talking about. His brown eyes flash into place, and he nods speculatively at me.

"You're still silver, but like blinding silver now. I figured your color would blend now that you've..." Ami gestures toward the bed. "But it's still one color. I'll have to look at Zeph and see what—"

"Ami, what do you know about Bonding Magic?" I ask, suddenly cutting him off.

Ami's eyes narrow ever so slightly. "Not much. What do *you* know about Bonding Magic?" he fires back at me.

I shrug. "I guess it was used to form the vow that created so many issues between the Ouphe and the Gryphons."

"Yeah, that's pretty common knowledge," Ami deadpans. "So common in fact that Gryphons hunted down possessors of that branch of magic and tried to force them to break the bond. You can see how well that worked out for them."

"Yeah, I guess that explains why most of them are dead now," I admit.

"Oh, you can't lay all of that at the feet of the Gryphons. The Ouphe in power also killed off a good portion of that branch of magic, making sure no one could reverse the power dynamic they were thriving off of," Ami explains.

"So it's pretty safe to say that anyone with Bonding Magic should keep it on the down low because they aren't the most popular around these parts?" I ask, without trying to sound like I'm asking.

Ami looks at me for a beat before answering. "Yeah, that would be an accurate conclusion to come to," he agrees with a snort. Ami pauses. "Why are we talking about this again?"

"No reason in particular. I'm just trying to understand the history here," I tell him nonchalantly as I step into my boots and lace them up. "What's the training plan for today?"

"I'm not sure. We should check in with Sutton and find out. I think you've got a better grasp on your gryphon, and your transitions will get better with time. You know better how to defend yourself, and it's time she did too," Ami tells me as we walk out to the balcony.

Wings press out of my back as we both climb up on the railing. Wind pushes at me, sending strands of my white hair dancing back from my face. Green trees and rocks surround me, and I glimpse the market far below me as I jump off the balcony. I dive down, chasing the adrenaline rush it invites before I flap my wings, bringing me up to crest the cliff. I hitchhike on a current, and a beaming smile takes over my face as I think about how far I've come. Pride fills me, and I wonder if I'll ever get used to my ability to do this. Ami leads me toward the training fields, where we both land with ease. I pull my wings back in and walk toward the gathering crowd. I make my way to the side and start to scan the group of people, looking for Sutton.

"Nice of you to join us, highblood," Loa sneers, and my searching gaze snaps to her.

"Where's Sutton?" I blurt, and Loa's eyes narrow at me.

"Unavailable," she snaps and turns back to the group of trainees. "Now, where was I before I was interrupted by the dirty blood? Ah, that's right... There are those of us that believe we should learn to fight in this form in the event that we can't shift and fight as we were meant to." Loa looks around the trainees, her stare intense and unblinking. "But when the Syta and Altern lead us to victory against the Avowed scum, we will be fighting as gryphons, as our true selves. Which is why I'll be taking over your battle training. The day of our liberation is fast approaching, and each and every one of us needs to be ready." Loa pauses dramatically and allows her words to sink in. "Now, I will demonstrate what skills are to be expected. Who would like to volunteer?"

No one is quick to raise their hands, and with one look at Loa's massive size, I don't blame them. She looks around the crowd innocently, and before her eyes even land on me, I know exactly what she's going to do.

"Highblood, let's see what *superior skills* your tainted insides have blessed you with." She waves me forward, and I shake my head at her obvious efforts to get under my skin.

I could try to explain to her that I don't have any skills when it comes to fighting in my gryphon form, but I can tell she knows that. She wants to hurt me, get back at me for not listening to her in the bathroom and embarrassing her in front of her leaders. The punishing glint in her eyes speaks volumes, and I nudge at a sleeping Pigeon inside of me.

"Um, Pidge, I'm pretty sure this bitch is about to slaughter us,

so if you don't want that to happen, then now would be a good time to wake the fuck up." Pigeon doesn't even stir.

Perfect.

I return my focus to Loa just in time to see her boulder of a fist coming for my head. There's absolutely nothing I can do to stop it, and my head explodes with pain as her knuckles connect to my cheek without warning. I twist and slam to the ground from the force of the blow, and full on fucking stars twinkle in my vision.

"Now, your first lesson of the day, and one every single one of you should already know, is to always be ready for an attack. We have to stay vigilant and be prepared for anything," Loa advises, and then she walks over and kicks me in the stomach.

Tears fill my eyes, and I feel a rib crack from her armored shit kickers. I grunt against the pain and spit out the blood pooling in my mouth from her sucker punch to my face. Loa bends over me and whispers.

"If you know what's good for you, you'll stay down and you'll stay away from Ryn."

My body vibrates with emotion, and Loa mistakes it for crying.

"Save your tears for someone who doesn't dream of your death."

I roll on to my back and stare up at her, laughter spilling out of my mouth. She looks at me cautiously, clearly concerned by my abnormal reaction.

"Thank you, Loa," I tell her, and her eyes dart from me to the trainees who are all silently watching the exchange. I laugh harder and grab at my throbbing side.

"For what?" she finally snaps at me, her eyes bouncing around, puzzled and concerned.

"For waking her up," I reply, and then as easy as breathing, Pigeon surges forward and snaps at Loa's face.

Loa squeals a very non-warrior like squeal of surprise and rears back, just avoiding Pigeon's hooked beak. We scramble to our feet and wait patiently for Loa to shift. We could pounce on her early, give her a taste of her own medicine, but we don't need to peck at the weak and stand on their corpses to feel better about ourselves.

I expect Loa's gryphon to be black like her hair, or maybe it's her shit-stained soul I'm expecting to be reflected in her fur and feathers. So I'm surprised when she shifts and her body is fawn-colored, and her barn owl looking head is the only thing that's black. She opens her maw to screech at us, but we're on her before she can make a peep. I slam into Loa with such force I feel it vibrate through the ground. We're two feral, deadly animals doing our best to tear the other apart, and we growl and snarl as we claw, bat, and snap at each other.

Loa and I separate at the same time, neither of us getting the advantage over the other. We circle each other, assessing and watching for an opening. Or at least that's what Loa's doing. Pigeon seems less analytical about it all and more balls to the wall. She puts our head down and goes full rhino and charges. Loa's beak digs into the base of one of our wings, but she lets go when we ram her into the trunk of one of the surrounding trees.

Loa rears up and swipes at us with a talon-tipped hand. She gets our cheek, but it doesn't stop us from sinking the talons of one hand into her armpit and snapping at her throat simultaneously. She screams and pummels us with her wings and her other free hand. Pigeon is doing her best to rip off her other arm by shredding up through her armpit. Loa tries to drop her body weight on top of us as she's realized that rearing up to challenge us didn't go so well for her.

We pull the talons out of her armpit to keep her from getting us on our back, and immediately charge her again, hoping we can get her on her side. Pigeon is fucking pissed. She doesn't give a fuck what kind of damage Loa is doing to us this close with her talons and clawed back paws. She knows she has the upper hand over Loa, that she's more dominant and ruthless in her efforts to protect and claim what is rightfully hers.

I choose not to take this time to point out that Ryn is a big boy and can easily protect himself, and he by no means belongs to us, because the last thing I need is a pissed off Pigeon who feels the need to teach me another lesson and ghost me. I'd hate to know first-hand what it feels like to have my head ripped off, which is exactly what Loa would do if Pigeon receded right now and left me here to deal with this on my own. Fuck knows none of these asshole trainees have done anything to intervene at this point, so I'm pretty sure their help would be nonexistent if Pigeon abandoned me.

"That's right, Pidge, he's fucking ours, and no hulk-assed bitch is going to take him away from us!" I scream internally, feeling no shame about egging Pigeon on. Whatever shuts this Loa bitch down once and for all is okay in my book. And I'd be down to ride Ryn's face before we leave as a thank you to Pigeon for beating this shit talking worm of a woman beyond all recognition. With that thought, I stand back and take a long hard look at my own brutal ruthlessness. I shrug and decide it is what it is, and check back into the fight.

Loa has a new gash where her hind leg meets her torso. Blood is pouring out of it just like the nice wound we gave her in the armpit, and Loa is obviously tiring. We have gashes on our face, shoulders and chest but nothing as deep and debilitating as Loa's injuries. Loa growls at us as we circle her again, but even she sees it for the empty threat that it is. Her fawn eyes are filled with fear and desperation as her body grows weaker with each drop of blood that splatters to the dirt and grass beneath her feet.

Loa shifts back into her other form, but if she thinks that will stop us from ripping her apart, then she's the queen of all dumbasses. She just made this a thousand times easier. Pigeon leaps for her, mouth open and ready to rip Loa in half. Just as we're about to close in on her, someone slams into us, and it throws us off our lethal trajectory. Pigeon manages to get a swipe of our talons into Loa as we're shoved away from her, and it throws Loa spinning out into the surrounding trees.

Pigeon roars a challenge to whoever intervened, and we scramble to face off with the asshole that just stole our kill. Our gaze lands on honey-colored irises surrounded by black feathers and a gray and black beak. I expect Pigeon to go all demure, like she normally does around Zeph, but apparently, by protecting Loa, he's crossed some kind of line with Pigeon, and she's beyond enraged.

About fucking time she saw past all the muscles and hotness.

Images flash through our mind faster than I can make out. I can't be sure, but I get the distinct impression they aren't coming from Pigeon. She does this weird growl chuff thing, and then I can see the speedy images that she's suddenly projecting.

Are Pigeon and Zeph talking to each other?

Pigeon steps in the direction that Loa's body disappeared in, and Zeph once again moves to get in our way. I wait for Pigeon to tell him off via the image share they seem to be doing, but instead she charges Zeph and swipes at him.

Well, this just fucking escalated!

Shock bleeds into me, and it slams up against Pigeon's fury. I don't know what Zeph just did, but it seems the rose-colored glasses that Pigeon always has on when it comes to Zeph just got smashed into a million pieces.

We're all claws, talons, and pissed off rage as Pigeon attacks Zeph. He bellows at us, and I can hear the *stop* in it. I'm with Pigeon on this though, Loa started it. She came for us. We have every right to deal with her exactly how we want to. If *we* had been losing, does Zeph really think Loa would have had mercy on us? Would Zeph have stepped in if it were Loa leaping to rip our head off? Yeah, not fucking likely.

Zeph uses his brute strength to push us away. Pigeon and I go skidding back, but as soon as we get our footing underneath us, we're rounding on him again. Gryphons move in front of Zeph, protecting him, and I recognize some of them as the kids I've been training with. Sarai's distinct diamond like markings on her face stand out to me as I face off with Zeph's new protectors. I scoff, irritated by their intervention.

What kind of leader hides behind children? He should be protecting them at all costs, not the other way around. I shake my head, my thoughts filled with disgust. Even Pigeon is judging all the shit that just went down. Well, fuck Zeph, and fuck these Gryphon eyas' too. Little shits were quick to step in to protect Zeph, but who stepped in to protect me and Pigeon when Loa started shit?

I shoot Zeph one last scathing glare before Pigeon and I spread our wings and fly the fuck away. I'm done with this shit and with these people, and for once, Pigeon completely agrees.

19

"*That weak bitch owes us some fucking clothes!*" I seethe to Pigeon as I get dressed.

I ignore the eyeroll I can feel Pigeon giving me and the distinct impression she's telling me, "Fat chance." Angrily, I pull my shirt over my head and curse the fact that I once again don't have any fucking shoes. My ribs give a twinge of protest at my movements, and I take a second to breathe through the flash of pain. *Stupid fucking Loa and her bully bullshit*, I grumble to myself as I trudge out of my room and head down in the direction of the kitchens. I get about half way there and veer off toward the hallway that leads down into the Ouphe-haunted level of the cliff castle. This time, there's no creepy little kid to coax me down here, and when I step off the bottom stair into the hallway, Nadi doesn't appear out of nowhere and guide me to where I need to go.

The sound of my bare feet on the stone floor echoes around me with each assertive stride I make down the hall in search of the entryway into Vedan. I find the large sealed stone doors and hammer my fist on them. There's no booming knock or really even much noise other than the impotent sound of my skin slapping against the rock, so I start to shout for Nadi instead. Nothing happens. There's no darkening of the hallway or dramatic green glowing effect, and for some reason, that makes me feel a little panicked. This was the only plan that I came up with in my efforts to say fuck you and get the hell out of the Eyrie of the Hidden.

"Nadi!" I shout at the sealed doors again, my desperation clinging to the symbols etched into stone. "Your fucking essence is required!"

I step back to look around and see if there's any other way to get in. Some of the symbols on the door are familiar. Maybe if I can just recall some of what my dad taught me before he died...

"Welcome, Daughter of the Shadows," Nadi greets me, interrupting my thought.

Her ghostly mouth and face appear inches away from me, and I jump, releasing a surprised squeak. I grab my chest and simultaneously glare at her as I recover from the shock she just gave me.

"You did that on purpose, didn't you?" I accuse, and Nadi shrugs.

"This job gets pretty boring," she admits casually, and I can't help the exasperated chuckle that escapes me at the unexpected sign of her sense of humor.

The stone doors scrape open, and Nadi gestures for me to follow her in. Once again as she steps over the threshold, she loses the translucent thing she's rocking and looks more solid. We make our way back to the overgrown gazebo, and I find myself taking in the ruins around me.

"Have you made a decision about what we talked about previously, Daughter of the Shadows?" she asks me serenely.

I pull my fascinated focus from my surroundings and sober, remembering why I sought her out.

"This whole vow breaking thing, how do I do that?" I ask.

"You have to speak it into existence," she answers vaguely.

"Yeah, you said that before, but how does that work?" I press. "I'm assuming I can't just announce *the vow is now broken* and it will be, right?"

"The words that shatter are lost to the Ouphe people now. You will have to find them and then speak them into existence."

I nod in understanding. "Okay, I'll break the vow," I tell her. "But I think in order to do that, I need to get home. I need to get through the gate so I can look through my gran's house. I'm positive there's stuff there that will help me make sense of all of this," I explain.

I see a hint of doubt in her features. *Shit. My plan isn't working.*

"I had a dream this morning about my dad. I was in trouble for using my ability on some neighborhood animals. I had bonded them to me, and I completely forgot that it ever happened until now," I divulge, as I stare at my hands and wonder just what I'm capable of. "My dad was teaching me to read your language as well as speak it, and I know he had to have books and things back at my gran's place that will help me remember how."

Nadi observes me silently for several beats. The quiet is borderline uncomfortable, but I bite my tongue and its need to fill the quiet with useless rambling, and wait. The longer she stares at me, the more worried I start to feel. If she can't help me get to the gate and figure it out, I just might be screwed.

"As I said before, child, the Ouphe will assist and support you in any way possible. As they were the keepers of the gates, they would be the best source of information on how to navigate them."

Well, shit. I was really hoping Nadi could just tell me. There's no way I can find the Ouphe in a land I know nothing about, with threats lurking around that I'll probably never see coming. That feels like a solid plan if my goal is getting murdered, but since I really just want to get home, this suddenly feels like a hard pass. I rub my hands over my face and heave an exasperated sigh.

"Nadi, I get lost in this castle; there is no way I will be able to just wander out into this world and hope to stumble upon the Ouphe," I explain and immediately start thinking through what my other options might be. Maybe Tysa can help me.

"You wouldn't need to go all the way to the Ouphe, child. I can send my essence to let them know to meet you at a rendezvous point. I would also supply you with a map so you would know exactly where you're going."

My head snaps up on the word map. *I'm a fucking idiot. How the hell did I not think of a map?*

"That could work," I admit, my voice reflecting the shock I'm feeling.

A cream-colored cloth appears in Nadi's grasp. "It will take half a moon cycle to get there, but when you do, a guide will be waiting for you."

"Just like that?" I ask, suspicion bubbling up inside of me. This feels too easy.

"I can offer no guarantees about the gate and how it works, but our people will help you to acquire all that you need to be successful. Our existence depends on it," Nadi explains.

It's not exactly the answer I was looking for, but at this point, it's probably my best bet. Fuck knows Zeph isn't keeping his promise to take me home, and I'd be stupid to think he ever will. Something is going on with him and the Hidden that he's not telling me about, and I'm just sitting here like a dodo bird, pretending I'm safe and not surrounded by self-serving assholes. It's time to pull my head out of the sand and start making shit happen for myself.

I take the cloth from Nadi's outstretched hand, and with that, Nadi disappears. I twirl around just to be sure she's not behind me or something, ready to freak me out again, but she's nowhere to be seen. Wind wraps around me like a cyclone, and I'm once again thrown out of Vedan's doors. I crash to the floor as the stone entrance seals itself, and I go full grumpy old man and shake a closed fist at the now closed archway.

"That's not funny, Nadi," I shout into the empty hallway, and my anger bounces all around me, ricocheting off the stone walls.

I hear the faintest tinkling giggle, and I glare at the air all around me. I push up onto my feet and dust myself off, grumbling about hiring the Ghostbusters and how Nadi will be sorry. I unfold the thin, very delicate feeling cloth in my hands and run my gaze over the images that are printed there. My eyes hone in on the Quietus mountain range. There is a purple spot on the map a few inches away from where the foothills start. I also notice the demarcation on the map for the Amaranthine Mountains. There is a green *you are here* dot, and I know that's exactly what it is as it's nestled on a cliff that has a big lake on the other side of it.

The Amaranthine Mountain range is surprisingly not far from where I am now. They're in the opposite direction that the purple dot is telling me I need to go. *Why am I such a bird brain?* Why did I think the Amaranthine Mountains were so far away? Zeph flew here with me after he attacked me. He wouldn't have been far from safety; wouldn't have risked his precious life and the lives of his pride by doing something reckless like fly where it's dangerous.

I fold up the map and lean against the stone wall. I could go to the Ouphe and see if they have any suggestions on how to get the gate to work. But if they don't, I could just end up in a similar or worse situation than I'm in now. Yeah, Nadi said they're *my people,* but who is she kidding; I have no people here. I'm too *highblood* for the gryphons and will probably be too gryphon for the Ouphe. I stare at the stone doors, lost in thought.

Or, I think to myself, I could just go to the gate on my own. Zeph and Nadi made it seem like I need some kind of ancient instruction manual to get it to work, but I sure as fuck didn't have anything like that when I was pulled into this world. I didn't do anything to get through the gate other than get electrocuted and knocked unconscious, maybe just my presence will unlock it? Or maybe when I get there, the *on* switch will be super obvious. Warmth fills me with that thought, and I decide that just going to the gate is the plan that makes the most sense. I mean, worst case scenario, if I can't get the gate to work, I can always go meet up with the Ouphe. No harm, no foul, and none the wiser.

Determination sweeps through me, and I fist the map in my hand and head for the stairs. First stop, the kitchen, to steal as much food as possible without getting caught.

* * *

"Where the fuck have you been?" snarls at me as I walk into my room, and I jump at the sound of it. If he hadn't just scared the shit out of me, I'd walk over and high five his use of the word fuck. He's getting good with it.

"What the fuck are you doing in here?" I demand as my eyes land on where Zeph is perched on my bed.

"I'm waiting for you," he rumbles, and the sound sends a fluttering of all kinds of yummy sensations through my stomach. He makes a similar noise right before he's about to come, and my body lights up with a fond remembrance of that fact. "We need to talk about what happened."

"No. You need to get the fuck out of my room!" I snap as I step all the way inside and shut the door behind me. I debate the best way to deal with the bag full of food I have my arm slung through. If I set it down, it will draw attention to it, but if I keep talking to him with it slung over my shoulder, he's bound to notice that too. *Shit.*

"It's not what you're thinking it is!" he defends, and I round on him like a boa constrictor does its prey.

"Oh it's not?" I ask with faux confusion and wide eyes. "You didn't step in and protect the weaker half in a dominance challenge?"

"No, I stepped in and stopped a training exercise gone wrong," he argues.

"Ahhhh, a training exercise. Is that what that was? Funny, I've never seen Sutton start beating on a trainee with no warning before," I point out, my voice dripping with imitation sugar.

As Sutton's name leaves my mouth, Zeph shoots off the bed, and a deep growling starts in his chest. I take a challenging step toward him.

"She attacked me without warning or provocation. She made it personal when she told me to stay away from Ryn and that she dreams of my death. I responded to her *challenge* with the same level of force that she would have if the roles were reversed. This was absolutely about dominance, and you stuck your beak where it didn't belong and probably just made things worse for me."

Zeph opens his mouth to say something and suddenly pauses. "What do you mean probably made it worse for you?"

"You think she's going to come for me head on now like she did today? No. That sneaky parrot will attack when I least expect it. And who the fuck knows when that will happen, but I can't watch my back around all the fucking people here who hate me, so she'll probably win. Are you going to step in and save me, Zeph?" I mock.

Zeph runs his hands through his long black curls and huffs. "I'll talk to her."

I snort a humorless laugh. "Good thinking. That'll definitely solve the problem." I drop the bag of food from my shoulder onto the ground discreetly, but Zeph's gaze immediately zeros in on it.

"What is that?"

"Nothing," I lie.

He breathes in a deep inhale, dousing my hope that he'll take my word for it. "Why do you have a bag of food?"

I watch his face morph into understanding as the question leaves his mouth. And he closes the distance between us. "Where the rut do you think you're going?"

"I'm going home. I don't belong here, and I don't want to be here anymore."

Pain flickers in Zeph's amber gaze, but it's quickly replaced by anger. "You told Ryn that you would stay here until he was back. You vowed," he accuses.

"No, I didn't, I just said I would, now I've changed my mind. I want to go home, and you promised you'd take me. So take me. I'm ready to leave."

"Your word means so little that you would say something and then go back on it just like that?" Zeph looks at me like I'm something gross he stepped in. Since he's practically been doing that since I met him, I remain unfazed by it.

I raise my eyebrows and give him my best *pot calling the kettle black* side-eye. "You're one to talk. Didn't you say something along the lines of when we get back here, you'll take me home?" I throw my hands out to punctuate my point. "And yet I'm still fucking here."

"That was before," he yells at me.

"Before what?" I yell back over all this cryptic bullshit all the time.

"Before you told Ryn you would wait."

I release a frustrated growl and push him. I have no Pigeon backing me up, so my efforts result in Zeph staying exactly where he is.

"Why do you fucking care? Why does Ryn fucking care?" I ask exasperated. "You hate me. Your people hate me. They spit on the ground as I walk by. They look at me like I'm the person solely responsible for all of their problems. You and Ryn avoid me at all costs unless the drive to get your dick wet is upon you. I mean, I get that, I really fucking do, but he can fuck some other chick in my absence. I'm certain it will make very little difference in the long run. This is just some fucked up powerplay with you guys. Some weird ass game of let's hatefuck the Ouphe tainted."

Zeph snarls at that, but I cut him off. "Oh please, did you not think I knew what was going on? I'm not stupid, and honestly, I don't fucking care. I got a good fuck out of it, but enough is enough. You and Ryn can tag team some other bitch. I'm done."

Zeph pulls me into him and grabs the back of my neck roughly. He brings his face down to mine and then rubs the scruff of his cheek against me as he nips at my earlobe.

"This has nothing to do with hatefucking or powerplays. And you *are* stupid if you believe any of the nonsense you just spewed. You have no idea how this world works or what's at stake."

I growl as I push away from him. He allows me to pull far enough back that I can look in his eyes but no further. "If I have no understanding of what's going on, it's because you've made it that way. You know where I come from and that I had no idea what I was or that this world even *existed* until you attacked me. But I don't see you filling in the gaps for me. I've had no lessons. No tutors to explain how gryphon life and this world works. You *want* me in the dark. Let's not pretend otherwise."

Zeph smashes his lips to mine, and I get lost in the feel of his brutal kiss for way too long before I boob punch myself and come to my senses. I try to push Zeph away, but he's not having any of it. He grabs my ass and tries to pull me up to straddle him. I fight to keep my feet on the ground, my head clear, and my senses free of Zeph and the molten effect he has on me.

"Zeph, stop." My protest is swallowed by his lips as he tries to coax me to open up to him.

Fuck, I want to. *Maybe just one more night of orgasms, and then I can leave tomorrow.* As that thought flashes through my mind, anger surges through me. The fucker's doing this on purpose. I bite his lip hard, and Zeph pulls back with a hiss.

"Stop," I demand, ignoring the fire and want in his eyes.

He leans forward, hell bent on ignoring my command.

"Tamod, Zeph!" I shout in his face. "I'm not trying to set up another round of catch-me-if-you-can rough sex. I'm serious. I can't fucking think with you kissing me and rubbing up on me," I scold, exasperated.

I register the frozen look on Zeph's face, and confusion flickers through me for a moment. I pale, and my blood runs cold as I realize that I just let that word fly out of my mouth like it's something I say every day. Zeph morphs from shocked to enraged, and I watch as all the affection he just had for me evaporates into nothing. His features shutter and harden, and I panic.

"Fuck, Zeph, I didn't mean…" I trail off and reach up to cup his face, needing him to feel in my touch as well as see in my face that I didn't mean to let that word slip out. My stomach drops when he flinches away.

What the fuck were you thinking, Falon? What the hell did you just do?

20

I stare into Zeph's betrayed gaze, and I instantly wish I could snatch that word out of the air, light it on fire, and eradicate its existence. I have no fucking clue why I said it. Maybe it was the echo of the dream I had this morning fucking with my good sense, but as I watch Zeph's eyes go from shocked to furious, I know this is a fuck up of epic proportions.

"How in all of the stars do you know that rutting word?" Zeph demands, his voice low and measured as he slaps my hands away from his face.

"How the fuck do you not know the meaning of *stop* and *no*?" I snap back, defensive.

"You like to fight me and then fuck me, Falon. I thought it was just more of the same." There's a deadly calm to him now that sets every hair on my body on end with alarm. He takes a menacing step toward me, his stare filled with fury and betrayal.

I want to deny what he just said, but I can't. It's true.

"Who are you?" he snarls at me, grabbing me by the arms and shaking me like he thinks if he does it hard enough, the truth will fall out at his feet.

"You're hurting me," I protest on a growl and try to shove him away.

"Good," he snaps at me, his eyes narrowed and filled with promises of more pain.

"How do *you* know *that word*?"

"My dad taught me," I confess on a shout, and his glare turns even more bitter.

"How sweet, your Ouphe father taught his little girl how to enslave and control the masses. What fun you two must have had."

"Fuck you, Zeph! I haven't said that word since I was little. You wouldn't stop—"

"So you thought you'd make me? Is that it?" Zeph accuses, cutting me off.

"No," I insist, but Zeph dismisses it with a hate-filled look.

"You forget, little sparrow, that I'm not Avowed. There's no magic running through my blood that would force me to obey you."

"I wasn't trying to force you," I defend, but the statement tastes bad in my mouth.

Was I?

"It just slipped out," I offer weakly, not even sure if I believe myself.

"It just slipped out," Zeph repeats, his hands shaking with the rage that suddenly surges through him.

"They used that word on my mother to keep her from moving while a group of guards forced themselves on her. They used that word on my father and older brother so they would have to stand still and watch. I was too young for the vow and the mark, too young to understand what was going on, but the screaming..." He trails off, his voice dripping with pain and buried emotion. "My mother was screaming, and they wouldn't let me go to her."

I'm horrified by what he's telling me, and I watch as the mountain of a gryphon in front of me melts away and leaves a traumatized little boy in his place. His eyes grow distant, and I fucking hate the memory that must be replaying in his mind right now. I want to rip it out of his mind and then rip the vocal cords from my throat so I can never speak another word that could ever conjure any remnants of what happened to him again.

"I'm sorry," I lament, and I step into him to try and offer comfort. I want him to feel the apology in every fiber of my body, and I want to rescue him from the brutal shadows that are haunting him right now.

He flinches back from my touch and rounds on me.

"Are you?" he challenges, and the question feels like a slap across my face. "Are you sorry that they cut her throat and then his? All because he spoke out against the vow and the highborn leaders who were abusing it. Are you sorry that my brother's mind broke, that he never came back from that night? That he wasted away to nothing and then died in my arms? Are you rutting sorry as you spew that word out so casually, as if my pain and my body are yours to command?" I flinch back as Zeph bellows the last sentence into my face, his pain and trauma like a punch through my chest.

"I didn't know," I tell him quietly, but it isn't true. My father warned me about words and their power the first time I used this word and froze the animals I was playing with. He told me about the responsibility that came with such a language, and then he died, and I stopped speaking it, stopped respecting it, and now here I am.

Zeph steps back from me, his chest heaving with the effort to rein in his emotions. "So, Falon Solei Umbra. Gryphon shifter who thought she was a wolf. Innocent female who just happened to be found by the Syta of the Hidden. Why would your father teach *you* these words? The words that someone with Bonding Magic uses to enslave others?"

His question rakes up my back like claws, and I flinch. I immediately think of the conversation I just had with Ami about Bonding Magic and what happens to the people who have it. I open my mouth to say *I don't know*, but Zeph's honey gaze sears through me, and as dumb as it may be, I don't want to lie to him, not like I've been lied to my whole life.

"Nadi said I was a Bond Breaker," I admit on a hesitant whisper, and Zeph's features war between confusion and horror.

"Who the rut is Nadi?"

"She's the ghost that lives in Vedan. I guess my blood woke her up," I explain, awkwardly hating that it makes me sound like a fucking loon. Hating the way that Zeph is looking at me like I'm something that needs to be eradicated, like I'm dangerous.

"Woke her up for what purpose?"

I swallow down the warning that zings through me to keep my fucking mouth shut and take a deep breath. "Um, she said something about how I could break the vow once and for all. Hence that whole Bond Breaker shit I just mentioned," I utter with way too many unnecessary hand gestures.

I suddenly can't seem to stop fidgeting. Maybe it has something to do with the possibility of the impending death that Zeph is currently breathing down my neck. Or maybe this is the first time I've really voiced what I've been told, and believe it.

He scoffs, and murder fills his eyes. "Bond Breaker or Bond Maker?" he accuses. "If you *can* undo the vow, then why haven't you?" he challenges with a disbelieving sneer.

"Because I have no fucking clue how to," I snap at him and then instantly regret it when he slams me up against the wall in response.

I grunt against the force of it and pant through the adrenaline that crashes through me because of his aggression. His hand rests threateningly on my neck, and he runs the tip of his nose up the side of my face. "I should rip you apart right now," he tells me on a growl, and I glare at him. "Do you know what will happen to you when this world finds out you have Bonding Magic? You'll be hunted, little sparrow. You'll be used, and then you'll be slaughtered when you've served your purpose or become too much of a threat. The Ouphe will come for you, the Hidden will come for you, and the Avowed will be right on their heels."

His breath caresses my face, his scent sinking deeply into my lungs, and I find myself oddly calm in spite of what he's saying to me. Pigeon makes a weird fucking cooing sound inside of me that has me giving her the side-eye. *Fucking weirdo.*

"Leave, Falon," Zeph orders suddenly, and the command pulls me from my focus on the way he feels pressed up against me.

"Leave," he snarls more forcefully when I don't budge. "Get home if you can, hide if you can't, and hope a Cynas gets to you before the Avowed can, or worse, the Ouphe dregs track you down."

I stare up at him in shock. "You'll throw me to the wolves, just like that?" I ask, hoping my incredulity masks the hurt in my tone.

"It's where your kind belongs." I try to push Zeph way from me, but he doesn't release his hold on my neck. "Oh and, Falon, if you ever come back here, I'll kill you myself."

Zeph squeezes my throat ever so slightly to punctuate

his threat, and then with that, he storms out of my room. The door slams shut with a loud boom behind him. And I stare at the dark wood barrier for way too long, not sure what to do. He's just given me permission to do the very thing I've been pushing for since I first woke up in this place. But his exit feels like it's just taken something vital inside of me with him, and I don't fucking know what to think about that.

Fuck him, and fuck this world.

I grab my bag of food from the floor and open the top of it. I walk into the bathroom and grab my pile of clothes, my eyes landing on my reflection in the mirror. The girl that stares back at me looks hollow, and I turn away, hating that the word *coward* bubbles up in my throat as I stare at myself. I shove my clothes in the bag, cinch it, and then tie it to my front. My wings burst out of my back, easy as breathing, and I'm reminded of the time I saw Ryn call his wings and then put them away just like this. I wanted so badly to do it as well as he did, and here I am.

I have the sudden need to say goodbye to Ami and to Tysa and Moro, but I know they'll have questions. Questions I just can't answer. I need to leave before the Syta asshole supreme changes his mind and decides my death is a better palate cleanser for him than my possible capture and torture.

I clear my throat in an effort to disengage the melancholy that's trying to settle in my chest and roll my shoulders. I pull the map that Nadi gave me out of the waistband of my pants and unfold it as I walk out onto the balcony. Cool spray from the waterfall kisses my cheek, and it feels like the farewell I find myself suddenly hesitant to say. The purple dot reaches out to me like a beacon, but I ignore it and focus in on the mountain range on the opposite side of the map.

Here's to hoping I can get that gate to open for me and that nothing scary tries to eat me before I can.

And with that, I leap off the balcony and fly out into the night.

21

I stare up at a massive red-purple boulder that feels like it's laughing at me. That could be the exhaustion talking, but even Pigeon is giving it the side-eye. I lie underneath its shadow and watch the sun wake up and kiss the rock good morning. It took us all night long to touch down in the foothills of the Amaranthine Mountains, and now that we're here, it's clear that there was one seriously important detail that I didn't factor in. The mountain range is huge. It's way bigger than it looked on the map, and I have no idea where the gate is located amidst the rolling hills and bald peaks. Pigeon seems confident that she'll recognize where we were flying when we first crossed over when she sees it, but I'm skeptical to say the least.

I sit up on a groan and dig through the backpack for the waterskin I stole. I take a deep pull and let Pigeon know we need to keep an eye out for a water source soon. My hand brushes the turquoise football shaped fruit I have hidden in my bag, and I shove away the thoughts of Zeph that suddenly bombard me. An image of Ryn pops up in my mind, and I release a weary huff.

"I know, Pidge, but what are we supposed to do? Zeph

told us to leave, and even if I wanted to say goodbye to Ryn, I have no idea where he is. We'll just have to cross our fingers that there are some hot eligible gryphon shifters back home," I tell Pigeon, hoping it will reassure her, but I can feel her pout and longing.

I rub at my chest and hope for my sake that Pigeon can let Zeph and Ryn go. I don't want to spend my future mourning the loss of guys who probably don't give two fucks about our absence. An odd chirping sounds off to my left, and I scan the area as I cinch the backpack and haul my tired body to its feet. I don't sense a threat, but I'm reminded that I'm in a strange land I know nothing about and should probably get back up in the air where it's safer.

Ebony wings thrust out of my back, and with more effort than it should take, I'm up in the air and looking for the best current to use as Pigeon and I start our search for the gate. Wind fills my wings, and I'm guided along into a leisurely glide as Pigeon and I look for any familiar landmarks. We fly like that for hours until my neck and back are aching, and we've both come to the conclusion that scouring these mountains could take weeks, if not months.

Pigeon flashes an image of a stream into my mind, and I look around our surroundings for the water that she's spotted. "Fuck yes, Pidge," I cheer and mentally wing five her as I spot the same stream snaking through the rocks and trees. We make our way over to it and trace the water's path in the air for a while until I spot a clearing in the distance that the stream borders.

"That looks like a decent place to land. Gives us some space to spot anything that might come at us." I show Pigeon, who fills my chest with warm agreement.

I drop down toward the trees, eager to land, tuck my wings into my back, and hopefully get some rest and refreshment, but just as I get closer to the clearing, I can suddenly make out some kind of makeshift camp that's tucked into the side and hidden by the trees until you're practically on top of it like I am.

Motherfucker!

I pull up, panic slamming through me and thankfully shoving away some of my exhaustion. I try to change directions and hope to fuck whoever is down there didn't just spot me, but a telltale screech sounds off behind me, and with a sinking feeling in my stomach, I know I've been spotted.

Pigeon nudges me, and I open up to her and let her take control. We shift mid-wing-flap and then look behind us to gauge what kind of threat we're dealing with. Five gryphons are now in the air and closing in. Zeph's final threat to me rings loudly in my ear, and I don't want to find out if he'd follow through on it. Pigeon angles us for speed and flashes through the sky, looking for a place that offers cover. We need somewhere we can lose them, because with all the flying we've been doing, there's no way we can outmaneuver them for long.

Warning growls and screeches reach out from behind us, making it clear that we're being hunted. We zip through the sky, but I can feel on the wind that one of our pursuers is gaining on the left. We veer to the right to avoid contact for as long as possible. The evasive maneuver seems to work, and Pigeon and I maintain our lead and continue to search for something that helps us get these fuckers off our tail. We round a mountain, and the bright flash of sun on water beams up at us. It's momentarily blinding and keeps us from seeing the webbed mass that comes shooting up into the sky until it's almost on us.

Pigeon shrieks and barely avoids the net, and I realize too late that we weren't outmaneuvering the gryphons chasing us, we were letting ourselves be herded by them.

Fuck! Another net comes screaming up into the sky, and by some miracle, Pigeon does this crazy tuck roll thing that keeps us out of its clutches. But as we recover from the epic dodge we just executed, a third net comes speeding for us, and this one hits its mark.

The net slams into us and wraps around us like a snake does its prey. Pigeon can't extend her wings to catch the current, and we start to fall out of the sky, careening toward the water. We're spinning as we fall, and the torque of it leaves me completely disoriented. One second I'm staring at the sky, the next I can spot the water we're about to crash into any minute now. We're rolling with such force that it steals all ability to make any sounds, and we can't even scream as the water's surface looms even closer, bringing with it promises of pain.

Pigeon and I crash into the water, and it hurts almost as much as when Zeph the sky shadow smashed us into the ground. The heavy net surrounding us immediately pulls us further down, and I feel the terror and panic that surge through Pigeon as we're dragged against our will toward the bottom. I yank on the tether that connects us, demanding Pigeon's attention, and try to pull her back into me. The squares of the net that's doing its best to drown us look big enough for me to try and fit through, but I have to get Pigeon to relinquish control so we can shift and I can try to get out.

I slam against her a couple times, and it finally gets her attention. She quickly hands me the reins, and we shift back into me. I work to untangle the dense net from around me, and I lose the bag that was strapped to my chest. The map flashes in my mind as the bag sinks out of reach, but losing the map will be the least of our problems if I can't get us out of the net. I'm just small enough to wiggle my way out through the mesh of the dense rope. I kick frantically for the surface of the water, my lungs burning and my head starting to swim with black spots.

I barely break out of the water before I gasp, breathing in air and water at the same time. I cough violently trying to purge my lungs of the lake I just aspirated. Strong arms pluck me from the rippling depths, but there's nothing I can do to free myself from my captor as I work to clear my lungs of water and fill them with air instead. I'm flown to the bank of the lake, and I continue to cough and try to take in my surroundings. I can tell by how Pigeon has receded inside of me that she's hurt, and I know that saving our ass is just up to me now.

I'm set gently on the sand of the shore, and I immediately reach back with my left hand and grab the junk of whoever is holding me. As expected, he drops his hold and reaches down to protect himself. This gives me the perfect opportunity to whirl around and punch him in the throat with my other hand. I'm up and sprinting away as he collapses in on himself, and I send up a silent thank you to Sutton and his training.

A massive gryphon slams down into the sand in front of me, and I shriek in surprise. I try to change directions, but another gryphon cuts me off. I stop and spin, looking for a way out, but I'm cut off by gryphons at every angle. A couple of them shift out of their gryphon form, and I take that moment to charge the smallest gryphon of the group. He snaps at me, which is exactly what I hoped for. I dodge his hooked beak, just barely, and land a punch to the side of his head.

I scream through clenched teeth as fire shoots up my hand into my arm. I feel like I just punched a fucking boulder. I lose the momentum of the attack as pain vibrates up my arm, and before the gryphon I assaulted can move to tear me apart, someone is pulling me away from him.

My arm is throbbing, but I unleash all of the fight left in me as I try to get out of the grasp of whoever is holding on to me.

"Caught a live one, didn't we now," an amused voice announces. Chuckles sound off around me, and I struggle even harder to break free.

"Go tell the commander we caught something interesting," the same guy orders, and the gryphon to my right pumps its wings and flies away.

"Highborn from the looks of it. Is she marked?" another voice asks, and I'm immediately shoved forward.

I'm bent over at the waist, completely naked thanks to the sudden shift into Pigeon earlier. Whoever is holding me is also naked, and I feel his limp dick skim my ass and start to grow firmer. I release a warning growl that goes ignored as someone brushes hair from the back of my neck and checks the skin there.

"No mark," the first voice declares, and I'm pulled back up. I'm brought face to face with another naked massive shifter who has long straight black hair, blue eyes, and a dimple in his clean shaven chin. He brushes the white strands of my damp hair out of my face, and his eyes light up with interest as he takes me in.

I snarl at him, but this only seems to amuse him. The guy holding me tries to stop my continued struggling to get out of his hold, and I wince when he yanks on my hurt hand. *Note to self, if we survive this, never punch a shifted gryphon in the face again.* The blue-eyed guy in front of me doesn't miss my pained response, and he reaches out and grabs my chin in an effort to make me go still.

"You'll just hurt yourself worse if you keep that up, flower," he chides, his eyes locked on mine.

I'm still not sure if staring contests with gryphons hold the same weight as they do with wolves, but I fix my

lavender gaze on him and refuse to look away. I stop struggling, the fight slowly leaving my body, and the absence of it
invites shock and exhaustion to flood me.

"That's a girl," he tells me, the firm grip he has on my
chin softening ever so slightly, but he doesn't let go. "Now
what's a pretty purple flower like yourself doing way out
here?"

His bright blue eyes run over my features like he's
searching for answers, and I internally cheer as he's the first
to break eye contact with me.

"You don't look like a rebel," he observes, picking up a
strand of my hair. "And yet you bear no mark."

I debate the best way to handle this situation. My initial
instinct is to stay quiet, but as I subtly pull in a deep inhale
of the blue-eyed shifter in front of me, it confirms my suspi-
cions. He has the windy lilac scent of a gryphon, but that
same hint of citrus that the hunters that captured me and
Zeph in the woods had. I thought maybe it was because
those gryphons were related somehow, but now I'm realizing that the citrus smell might be what the vow does to a
gryphon's scent.

These shifters are the Avowed, and maybe, just maybe,
the truth of how I got here will work on them like it did with
the Hidden. I stare into the curious blue eyes of the shifter
in front of me and hope they don't have an Ami that will see
the parts of my story that I'm hiding. I'll just have to deal
with that later if it happens.

"My name is Falon Solei Umbra," I offer. I take a second
to look around at the strange gryphons surrounding me and
let fear and confusion leak into my eyes. "I woke up in this
strange place a couple of days ago, and I've been trying to
figure out how to get back home ever since."

"And where's home, flower?" Blue Eyes asks me, concern

leaking out of his tone, but it does little to mask the cunning glint in his eyes.

"Colorado."

A large tan gryphon slams down onto the sand on my right, and the force with which he lands sends vibrations through the ground up into my legs. His arrival pulls my thoughts away from the plausible cover story I'm trying to pull from my ass. This must be the commander that Blue Eyes requested. That thought turns to ash in my mouth as another massive, well-muscled shifter touches down gracefully on the bank just behind Blue Eyes. Large gray and white wings give a quick flap and are then quickly folded back, giving me a clear line of sight at a familiar face. My eyes go wide with shock and then quickly narrow with stupefied confusion.

What the fuck is Ryn doing here, and why does he smell different?

The end of book one

ALSO BY IVY ASHER

The Sentinel World

THE LOST SENTINEL

The Lost and the Chosen

Awakened and Betrayed

The Marked and the Broken

Found and Forged

SHADOWED WINGS

The Hidden

The Avowed

The Reclamation

MORE IN THE SENTINEL WORLD COMING SOON.

Paranormal Romance

HELLGATE GUARDIAN SERIES

Grave Mistakes

Grave Consequences

Grave Decisions

Grave Signs

THE OSSEOUS CHRONICLES

The Bone Witch

Book 2 coming soon

Shifter Romantic Comedy Standalone

Conveniently Convicted

Dystopian Romantic Comedy Standalone

April's Fools

IVY ASHER

Ivy Asher is addicted to chai, swearing, and laughing a lot—but not in a creepy, laughing alone kind of way. She loves the snow, books, and her family of two humans, and three fur-babies. She has worlds and characters just floating around in her head, and she's lucky enough to be surrounded by amazing people who support that kind of crazy.

Join Ivy Asher's Reader Group and follow her on Instagram and BookBub for updates on your favorite series and upcoming releases!!!

f facebook.com/IvyAsherBooks

⊙ instagram.com/ivy.asher

ⓐ amazon.com/author/ivyasher

BB bookbub.com/profile/ivy-asher